J. H. Rosny, known also as J. H. Rosny *Aîné*
meaning the elder, is one of the real pioneers of
modern science fiction and particularly of the
novel of lost races and primitive men which was
to culminate in Edgar Rice Burroughs' immortal
classic, *Tarzan of the Apes*. Rosny's caveman
novel, *La Guerre du Feu*, published in 1909,
is the only major work of his still in print in
English.

> *The Astonishing Adventure of Hareton
> Ironcastle* is the most "Tarzanic" of his
> lost race novels, and though continually
> in print in France and other European
> nations, it has never been previously
> published in English.

Now Philip José Farmer, author of the famous
Riverworld and *Ancient Opar* novels, has un-
dertaken to make available the essence of Ironcastle's marvelous safari into a lost African valley inhabited by unknown apelike races and the
weird life of an interstellar intruder. He has
told it in his own words, following Rosny judi-
ciously and adding certain surprising embellish-
ments of his own.

"Two peculiar animals appeared . . ."

IRONCASTLE

by J. H. Rosny

Translated and retold in English
by PHILIP JOSÉ FARMER

Illustrated by Roy Krenkel

DAW BOOKS, INC.

DONALD A. WOLLHEIM, PUBLISHER

1633 Broadway, New York, N.Y. 10019

FIRST PRINTING, MARCH 1976

3 4 5 6 7 8 9

 DAW TRADEMARK REGISTERED
U.S. PAT. OFF. MARCA
REGISTRADA. HECHO EN U.S.A.

PRINTED IN U.S.A.

TABLE OF CONTENTS

List of Illustrations

1.

The Gun Club

The Gun Club at No. 21 Union Square, Baltimore, Maryland, houses one of the most curious organizations in the world.

It is also the best known. Other clubs have existed for a much longer time. One scarcely needs to be told of Boodle's, the Garrick, the Diogenes, the Carlton, and the Reform Club. The latter is especially famous, since it was from it that Phileas Fogg, in 1872, started on his famous eighty-day dash around the world.

These clubs, as it happens, are British. But the Baltimore Gun Club, needless to say, is American.

It was founded during the Civil War. Or, as Southrons prefer, the War Between the States.

Its membership was restricted to those who had designed a cannon or at least a firearm of some description. No president of this organization or any member of the governing board had ever designed any weapon weighing less than five hundred pounds.

Artillerists had, from the beginning, formed the great majority of members. All but a few had been or now were professional military or naval men.

At the moment, in the year 1920, the Gun Club reported in its ranks only one amateur. Moreover, he was not nor had ever been enlisted in any army or navy in the world. He was a naturalist, the only one of his profession elected in the rather exclusive club. A number of members had actively opposed his election. Why should the inventor of a mere airgun—not a firearm by any stretch of technical de-

scription—be admitted into the august lists of cannon de-
signers?

However, his backers claimed that the airgun had seen
such service, and become so famous, that Hareton Ironcastle was a logical candidate for membership. Moreover, he
had a worldwide reputation as an explorer. And he did
come from an old and aristocratic Baltimore family. He
was descended from the Calverts and related to an eminent
Baltimore divine and scientist, Professor Porter. He had
demonstrated the effectiveness of his weapon against the
brobdingnagian reptiles and mammals of Maple White
Land in South America.

The man who carried the flag for Ironcastle was the
well-known surgeon and explorer, Dr. Savage. He had accompanied Ironcastle on the expedition to the fabulous
plateau first reported by Professor Challenger and described in detail by the British journalist, Edward Malone.
Dr. Savage's photographs showed how effectively the airgun operated against the stegosaurus and tyrannosaurus
rex. It cast a missile attached to thin electric wires which, in
turn, were connected to powerful electrical batteries. On
entering the body of the target, the wires delivered a massive voltage that stunned the monster. This enabled the
hunters to approach the fallen beast and pump a preserva-
tive into its body. Thus, an animal long thought extinct
could be brought back to civilization without damage to its
tissues. And there it could be dissected and studied under
ideal conditions.

Ironcastle and Savage had planned to transport their
specimens, each weighing many hundreds of tons, by floating them out in Zeppelins. It was not their fault that the
plateau was suddenly subjected to one of the greatest volcanic eruptions of historical times. The specimens were destroyed, along with all the animal and most of the vegetable life of Maple White Land. Hareton and Savage had
been fortunate to escape with their lives and with a few
photographs.

Of course, there were those who claimed that the photographs were faked, just as there were those who claimed
that the pterodactyl which Challenger had brought to Lon-

don was only an ingenious clockwork mechanism. But then there are too many in this modern age who still insist that the earth is flat. And this despite the irrefutable proof offered by Misters Barbicane, Ardan, and Nicholl on their return from their journey around the moon, so vividly described by Monsieur Jules Verne.

At the moment, Hareton Ironcastle was seated in the great library-sitting room just off the vast meeting hall of the Gun Club. From his chair he could see, through the doorway, part of this impressive and unique room. Is it necessary to repeat here what the whole world has read about in Monsieur Verne's excellent narrative? The lofty pillars formed of cannons, mounted upon giant mortars as bases? The trophies of blunderbusses, matchlocks, arquebusses, carbines, etcetera, all picturesquely interlaced against the walls? The candelabras formed of muskets bound together? The platform on which the president and the governing board sat during the assemblies? The president's chair, supported by a gun-carriage, modeled after a 32-inch mortar, pointed at an angle of ninety degrees, suspended upon trunnions? Or his table, a huge iron plate supported upon six carronades, holding an inkstand made from a beautifully chased Spanish piece, and the sonnette, used during the often violent debates to emit an explosive report which would bring the meeting to order?

No, it is not.

At the moment, Ironcastle was reading the latest copy of *The American Journal of Arctic Explorers*. He was a very tall, muscular man with a long yet rugged and quite handsome face. His eyes were Viking sea-green. Though forty-three, he had a skin as smooth and as pale as a young girl's.

He heard a cough and looked up from an article on the recent discovery of descendants of the ill-fated Franklin expedition. A servant was standing there.

"Pardon me, Mr. Ironcastle. Mrs. Storm says that it is time to dine."

"Thank you, Graves."

Ironcastle ignored the servant's faint expression of disapproval. Graves was an old-timer, very conservative, and he had not adjusted to the presence of women in the club. Though they were not permitted beyond the dining room and the associated waiting room, they were, according to some members, a disrupting influence. Cannons and their history and their future use were fit subjects for males only. Who could engage in a serious discussion when the chatter of women reached even into their library? Who knew what they would next demand in their incessant and increasing demands for equality? One day, some woman would design a cannon, no doubt trimmed with lace, and demand membership on the basis of this. Then what? The world was changing all too swiftly and all for the worst.

Hareton smiled slightly and walked across the room and into the dining room. He had no presentiment that this day was any different from others. His thoughts were of the northern regions, of ice and snow, not of blazing suns and green jungles, of nightmare trees, beasts, and manlike beings.

2.

A Fantastic Land

Rebecca Storm waited for the spirits to talk through her. The gold pencil she held lightly above the blank sheet of paper waited also. If a ghostly voice spoke in her head, it would move the pencil, and she would write. But, so far, she had heard nothing, not even a whisper.

"I'm a mediocre medium," she said, and she sighed. She looked across the room into the mirror and saw an elderly woman with a camel's face and camel-colored hair. Her eyes were large and bright, those of a visionary, her only attractive feature. But her teeth were large and ugly, hyena-like. Had they scared off even the spirits?

"Am I unworthy?" she murmured. "Have I lost merit in the Almighty's eyes? If so, why?"

Whatever the reason, the spirits did not care to communicate with her today. She rose and headed for the dining room as a clock chimed.

Hareton Ironcastle, her nephew, entered. She said, "Hareton, what does *epiphenomenon* mean? It sounds blasphemous!"

"It's philosophical blasphemy, anyway, Aunt Becky."

A young woman sitting at a table looked up from her grapefruit. She had a body that could only be described as statuesque. Her hair was many-hued: amber, honey, and rye.

"What does that word mean, Father?"

"It means, Muriel, that if you had no conscious mind, you'd be about to eat your Virginia ham and would be asking this same question. Only you wouldn't know you were eating the ham or asking that question. In other words, epi-

phenomenal consciousness exists in tandem with your
body, but there is little or no connection between the two."

Rebecca Storm said, violently, "Surely, philosophy
couldn't have invented such absurdities?"

"Yes, Aunt, philosophers have and will. That's the business of philosophy, to invent absurdities which, after all,
may or may not be true."

"They should all be locked up in insane asylums."

"Their insanity may be what keeps the rest of us sane."

The maître d'hotel brought in some eggs and smoked
pork for her. Hareton, who disliked eggs, was served
grilled meat and two small sausages. A teapot, rolls, butter
and pots of jam were added to the breakfast. The three
guests pitched in and ate without further discussion. Hareton was finishing his last roll with jam when the mail was
brought in. Rebecca pounced on two letters and a newspa-
per, *The Church.* Hareton grabbed *The New York Times,*
the *Baltimore Mail, Washington Post, New York Herald,*
and a letter and a telegram. He opened the latter, smiled,
and said, "The nephews from France will be visiting us."

"I detest them," Rebecca said.

"But Monique is fascinating," Muriel said.

"Like the necromancer who took on the shape of a
young girl," Rebecca said. "I cannot see her without feeling strangely affected. She attracts, yet repels."

"There's something in what you say," Hareton said.
"However, if she seems frothy, she is also deeply loyal to
those she loves."

The envelope bore the stamp of Gondoroko, an African
country still little explored even in 1920. From it he took
out another envelope. This was rotting and dirty, covered
with the legs and filmy wings of crushed insects.

"It's from our poor friend, Samuel. It stinks of the desert, the jungle, the swamp."

He opened it and read, enigmatic expressions passing
over his face. Before he had finished its many pages, he
was breathing harshly.

Finally, he put it down. "I don't know. It sounds like
one of H. Rider Haggard's fantastic romances."

Muriel said, "For heaven's sake, Father! What is it all about?"

"I can't tell either of you unless you give your solemn word not to reveal its contents to anyone. Otherwise. . . ."

"Otherwise, we'll die of curiosity," Muriel said. "Of course, I give my word."

"And you, Aunt?"

"Yes, I give my word."

Hareton, though usually remarkably self-controlled, was obviously excited. Muriel would have known that this was no ordinary letter even if he had said nothing about it.

"You know that Samuel Darnley went to Africa to search for new plants. He hoped that the discovery of these would validate his theory. What he called his *theory of circular transformation*. He went into the interior of Gondoroko, where few men, native or European, have gone. His letter came from there."

"Who brought it out of there?" Rebecca said.

"A black. He carried it to a British outpost. And it was mailed from there in a new envelope."

Hareton seemed to withdraw into himself. His eyes looked empty.

"But," Muriel said, "what does Mr. Darnley say about it?"

Suddenly Hareton came out of his reverie. "Ah, yes! What did he find there? He found things that seem to exist nowhere else. The plants and the beasts, he says, differ fantastically from those in any other land."

"They're stranger than those found in Australia?"

"Far stranger! He says that it's almost like being on Mars! He says that sometime in the distant past, perhaps millions of years ago, a series of cataclysms of unknown nature struck the area. It's about a third the size of Ireland, you know. That's not a large area for the vast country of Africa. But it's very difficult to get into it, and apparently even more difficult to get out of. It's taboo country for most of the tribes who live near it.

"Anyway, it's populated by mammoth beasts and reptiles unknown to science. He says, and I know you'll think

he's crazy, that there are warm-blooded reptiles* there!
There is also a mammal which may be as intelligent as
man. But . . . the plants . . . he says . . . I don't really know what he means . . . are extremely complicated in
anatomical structure. And they're able to hold men in
check! What does that mean, *hold men in check*?"

"That smells of witchcraft, black magic!" Rebecca said.

Hareton smiled slightly. "Must you always interpret everything as supernatural, Aunt?"

Muriel asked, "Does Mr. Darnley actually say that the
plants are *intelligent*?"

"He doesn't say that. He does say that they have mysterious faculties, none of them resembling our cerebral ca-
pacities. Whatever that means. But he states that they can,
somehow, defend themselves. And conquer!"

"Can they move around?"

"No. But they can extend themselves, grow, at an incredible rate. Which makes them, in a sense, mobile."

"This Samuel Darnley is mad," Rebecca said. "Or else
he's fallen under the power of Satan."

"There's only one way to find out," Hareton said. "Go
there and see for myself."

Rebecca said, "You can't mean it? You're not going
there? To join that lunatic creature?"

"I'll do just that, Aunt Becky. Or at least try to do it.
He's expecting me."

"And you would abandon your daughter just like that?
Leave her unguarded with so many young men around
her? Not all of whom, I'm sure, have honorable inten-
tions!"

Muriel laughed and said, "This isn't 1880, Aunt Rebecca. I can take care of myself."

She paused, then said, "Anyway, I want to go with Father."

Hareton, startled, said, "Into the desert, the jungle, with
all its dangers? You must. . . ."

"If I were your son, you wouldn't object. Am I not as

* This would have seemed incredible in 1920 or even in 1974. But
see *Dinosaur Renaissance*, R. T. Bakker, *Scientific American*, April,
1975. P.J.F.

well trained as any man? Didn't I keep up with you in Arizona, the Rockies, Alaska? Have I ever been a burden to you in your travels?"

"No," Hareton said. "But you *are* a girl, Muriel."

"That argument is out of date. Look, Father, you'll be gone at least two years. I'll miss you too much, worry about you. No, I want to go with you. I *will* go with you."

"Muriel," he whispered. He was moved at her concern yet angry with her.

Graves reappeared, bearing a card on a silver plate. Hareton picked it up and read, aloud: "*Phillippe de Maranges*. But there's another name pencilled on it. *Et Monique*."

He rose. "Let's go see them."

"Don't be so happy at this interruption, Father," Muriel said. "You can't avoid answering me."

Hareton ignored her. He strode out of the room, followed by the two women. They found a young man and woman in the lobby. Phillippe de Maranges was a tall striking-looking man with a strong face and black eyes like hot lava. However, Monique was attracting all the attention of the other guests.

"Delilah must have looked so," Rebecca thought.

Hareton greeted them and then asked questions. The European accepted the American's directness. He was used to him.

"Why have I come here? The reason is simple. I must go into business."

"Why?" Hareton asked.

"Mainly because of Monique. Our father left us an inheritance with great debts and income too uncertain."

"I fear, my dear boy, that you are not gifted for business. You'd have to consult a specialist with whom you could discuss your capital. I see no chance of that in Baltimore. Perhaps my nephew, Sydney Guthrie, could handle you. Personally, I am ridiculously inept at business."

Phillippe sighed and said, "I know I don't have the knack for it. But since I have to do something. . . ."

Maranges did not seem unduly concerned. He looked at Muriel as if he would like to scoop her up in his arms and

run off with her. Hareton wasn't bothered by this. Most
young men seemed to have the same idea. And then he
thought, perhaps I *should* take her along. Balance the dangers of her being unchaperoned here against those of Africa. No, he was being the overprotective, perhaps jealous,
father. She could be trusted; she could, as she said, take
care of herself.

"You're far better suited to a perilous, exciting life in
exotic places than trying to be a businessman in Baltimore," Hareton said to Maranges. "War has made you
used to hardships. I have something in mind suited to your
talents. Could you endure the privations of a Burton, a
Stanley, or of your Marchand?"

"I've always dreamed of such a life."

"Dreams, when confronted with reality, often turn into
nightmares. You'd be encountering intense discomfort,
cannibal tribes, fatigue, fever, poisonous insects, God
knows what else."

"Do you think it's comfortable to freeze at an altitude of
five thousand meters in a Spad? A flying machine which is
both frail and capricious? Or that the fevers or lions are
more dangerous than the Boche? I am ready to
go . . . under one condition . . . that the adventure will
make Monique financially secure."

"I can't guarantee anything except suffering. It is true
that the country where I'll be going is supposed to contain
much gold and silver, emeralds and diamonds. But that is
only rumor, though the explored part of Gondoroko is rich
with valuable minerals, so it can be presumed that the
unexplored part is also rich. It's also full of living treasures,
but those won't interest you. With good luck, you may suc-
ceed in getting a fabulous dowry for Monique. On the other hand, your bones may dry in the desert or rot in a
swamp. Think it over."

"I'd be stupid to hesitate. Only, would I be a handicap
to you?"

Hareton said, "You're a fine shot, Phillippe. Anyone
who's shot down thirty-three Boches, some of them Ger-
many's finest, is cool and capable. I need reliable men of

high caliber. I intend to take Sydney Guthrie also . . . he's in Baltimore now . . . you two would be invaluable."

"You said something about living treasures?"

"Forget about them. They aren't your concern."

Hareton again seemed to withdraw into himself.

3.

The Unrelenting Night

Darkness was just about to cover the ancient forest. The beasts that fed at day were bedding down; those that ate nocturnal animals were stirring. Both moved slowly though not always quietly under the trees, the ancient unfeeling, uncaring kings of the shadowy kingdom.

Branches cracked in a dense region of the forest. A hairy being, after dropping from a baobab, stretched out on the ground. His four dark hands were clenched like fists.

He looked like the shambling, low-browed half-beast that had brought fire to the ancient darkness. But his jaws and thickly matted chest were more like a lion's.

He lay there for a long time, caught in the net of a dream where the past was a shadowy fog and the future unthinkable. Finally, he called out, managing to sound both harsh and soft. Out of the darkness came four creatures. They were females with the same dark brutal faces, the same hands like feet and feet like hands. Rays of sunlight, filtering through their many-branched heaven, lit up strange yellow eyes. Following them were six young, playful and noisy, still not ready to huddle together for the long night's sleep.

The male rose, stood on his feet, hooted, and led his band to the west where a vast red sun died. They went through the jungle for awhile, the young bounding, tumbling, wrestling with short sharp cries. Suddenly, the male halted. He uttered a low growling warning, and the young, as if their lips were tied to a single string yanked by the male, became silent and motionless. The male moved quietly now, his band behind him, until he was close to the edge of a small clearing.

Here he got down on all fours, crawled, stopped, and looked into the clearing from behind a bush. He saw a few burned-out tree stumps and some ferns and grassy plants.

He also saw fire. Not the unchecked fire generated by lightning. Fire controlled by creatures that walked upright on two straight legs. They stood or sat unperturbed by the flames, flames fed further by boughs dropped by the creatures. The fire grew as the sun died. And as the dusk also died, the fire became more alive, pink, then scarlet. It lit up a number of four-legged beasts, large-humped, long-necked creatures and small horned bleating things.

A rumbling came from the bushes at the opposite end of the clearing. The fire-creatures stopped their chattering, looked across the clearing. One resumed chattering then, and the others seemed to become relaxed. But several stood turned toward the source of the growling, holding peculiar-looking sticks in their hands.

There was no wind, so the male could not smell the beasts that had growled. But he recognized the noise. There were lions crouching in their cover. Now and then, the fire shone on their eyes, outlined briefly the monstrous heads. It was not safe to linger there, but he made no move to withdraw. A silent order had come down from the forest, from the ancient kings. He was to stay here; perhaps, if he were commanded, attack.

The lions would not know fire. They had never seen it run through the dry grass or devour the kings. They knew only the frightening lightning that came with the storms. But they feared the throbbing flames; their instincts told them that here was mightier force than they. Yet they, too, stayed by the edge of the clearing.

And, as the great ape watched, he saw one creep out into the light. They also were under orders. Nothing else would have forced them to come nearer this unknown danger.

The male ape knew about fire. Three times he had encountered it, the living nonalive that roared and growled and grew unchecked. In his dull memory pictures flowed:

thousands of forest creatures, bounding in silent panic, the beating of thousands of wings. He himself bore arm and chest scars; they had healed but he still woke up screaming sometimes from the undying memories of unendurable pain.

Inside the fence of boughs thrown up in a circle around them, the strange beings watched the approaching lion. There were fifteen men as black as the great ape and seven men and a woman with pale skins.

A tall man with blond hair yelled, "Don't shoot!"

The other cats, a male and two females, came out then. Their leader roared. The second male came up even with him; the lionesses separated, one going to the left flank, the other to the right.

At the same time, a man looked behind him and saw the heads of the great apes above the bush. He shouted something. The others turned, the woman gasped loudly and some of the blacks moaned.

"Don't shoot!" the blond man said again. "It's unlikely the lions'll attack. As for the gorillas, it's even less likely."

"Improbable, no doubt," a white man holding a rifle said. "I don't think they'll come this near the fire . . . yet."

One of the blacks spoke rapidly in his native language. The tall blond replied in the same tongue. Then he said in English, "He can't understand what lions are doing here. They're savannah creatures, not jungle dwellers. They shouldn't be here."

He looked behind him again, then turned for a longer look. "They're as big as gorillas! But they're not gorillas!"

"Ten guns and a Maxim," a giant said. He had granite jaws and green eyes speckled with amber and copper. His hair was lion-colored. He was Sydney Guthrie, Hareton's nephew.

The two male lions roared at the same time as they took another step forward. The apes started, their hair bristling. They wondered why the bipeds did not flee. Were they prisoners, unable to get out of the high-piled fence of boughs?

One of the blacks pulled the lever of the Maxim .45 caliber machine gun. Guthrie aimed his loaded elephant rifle at the lead cat. Phillippe de Maranges, sure of his aim, kept an eye on the second lion. The men were not frightened; their pulses were beating swiftly but with controlled excitement. This was the peak of life, the moment when life might be taken away.

A black spoke sharply. They turned to see the huge male ape advancing into the clearing. But the humans were not his goal. He was going around the *boma*, obviously intent on attacking the lions. As he neared them, he roared, exposing large teeth. He lacked, however, the long sharp canines of the gorilla.

"No known ape has teeth like that," Hareton said.

"Is he crazy?" another white man said. He spoke with a British accent, and his handsome features looked much like those of the poet, Shelley.

"I don't know," Hareton Ironcastle said. "No gorilla would act like that. But then he isn't a gorilla, as I said."

The ape stopped, bent, plucked up a few blades of the sparse grass, and blew them into the air.

"That's gorilla behavior," Hareton said. "Definitely an aggressive gesture. But he's not bluffing. If he were, he'd have stayed closer to his band."

The ape moved forward. His instincts told him to flee but his body moved toward the confrontation. The kings had ordered this, and there was no disobeying them. Why had he been told to attack the bipeds only to have that order countermanded a moment later? And this directive to attack the lions instead, why had it come?

Dark sluggish vegetable thoughts coiled through his brain. He had no words for orders to attack, but they had come, and he would obey.

Suddenly, the big lion in the lead charged. Roaring, it ran past the *boma* and leaped into the air. As it came down, it seized the ape with its front paws. Then the two were rolling on the ground.

"Oh, save him, save him!" the girl cried.

Hareton looked at her curiously. "Why?"

"He seems so human!"

Maranges tried to aim at the lion, but the rolling bodies made accuracy impossible. The ape, though torn and bleeding from claw and tooth, his entrails hanging out, had gotten on the lion's back. Now he locked his arms around the huge throat, his hands clenched, and pulled back. The giant cat roared and rolled, trying to roll over so he could crush his rider. He only succeeded in flopping on his side, with the ape's legs still around his body, the massive arms closing on his throat. Suddenly, the roar was cut off. The lion struggled, his legs kicking, while his eyes popped out.

"Watch it!" Hareton said. He lifted his rifle, and it exploded. A lioness, bounding toward the pair to help her mate, fell. She did not get up again.

"Fire at the other lions!" Hareton said. But he told the machine-gunner, "Hold your fire!"

Maranges hit the other male in the neck, and the cat crumpled. The female turned to run, and Guthrie's bullet caught her in a leg. Limping, she raced into the bush and was gone.

They turned to the struggling pair. The lion gasped as it fought for air. The ape, growling, his yellow eyes bright in the fire, strained. Suddenly, it was all over.

The ape loosed his hold and crawled away, his entrails dragging on the ground. The humans were silent, for a moment. It was as if they had just witnessed, not a battle between two beasts but one between beast and man. Hareton's voice spoke for them when he said, "Why shouldn't our remote ancestors have had the strength of this anthropoid?"

"Can't we help him?" the girl said.

The Englishman, Sir George Curtis, baronet, spoke. "We can at least see what we can do for the poor beast."

Guthrie lowered his Bland's .577 axite express. He said, "Let's go."

Ironcastle shouted to the blacks to bring some torches. Though the fire lit up the clearing, it did not penetrate the bushes beyond. He was not sure what else might be hiding in the darkness. This was Africa, which he knew well. But it was, in a sense, not Africa. They were in a weird clime, where some of the wonders were terrifyingly alien.

The female apes had been slowly approaching the wounded male, uttering soft chirruping cries. When the blacks tore down a part of the *boma* for a passage, they stopped. They looked with large yellow eyes, wondering what the bipeds intended to do. When the men emerged, they turned and ran back into the bush. But their eyes glowed yellowly just within the forest.

By the time they reached him, the male had quit trying to crawl away. He lay on his back, gashed, bloody, the intestines lying partly on the ground. He turned his head as the men neared but he made no other move, uttered no sound. When they were within a few feet, he closed his eyes and his mouth fell open.

"Nothing we can do for him," Sydney said. "Besides, what use could he possibly be to us?"

"No *use*," Maranges said. "But would you ask a human being what use he was if he were in this terrible condition?"

"I really feel that he is a human being," Muriel said in a low voice.

Hareton, looking startled, said, "What are *you* doing here? You shouldn't be here. Get back into the *boma*."

"Nonsense, Father. With all of you around me, I'm just as safe here as in the *boma*. Besides, I want to see this . . . creature . . . close up."

Hareton shrugged and said, "All right. I keep forgetting I promised to treat you just like a man."

He looked around. "Anybody got a small mirror?"

They all looked at Muriel. She shook her head. Maranges said, "I have one in my pocket." He handed it to Hareton, who got down on his knees beside the ape.

"Be careful!" Guthrie said. "It could kill you with one blow."

"It's intelligent enough to know I'm trying to help it," Hareton said. "I think. . . ."

He slowly brought the mirror close to the ape's mouth.

"He looks dead. But he isn't."

He showed them the faint mist on the glass.

"How could he be revived? How could he bear those awful wounds?" Maranges said. "And look at the blood. He must have lost many quarts."

"Couldn't we give it a try?" Muriel asked.

Hareton said, "We can do that. If he were a man, I wouldn't give him a chance. But the vitality of these brutes is incredible."

Four blacks, two at each arm, dragged the five-hundred-pound creature inside the barricade. The gap was closed, and Hareton opened the medicine box.

"We can disinfect and dress some of these wounds," he said. "The others will have to be stitched up. But, first, the guts."

He looked up at Muriel. "Do you think you could stand helping me? I could use another sewer."

"I can do just about anything a man can. And I won't faint on you."

"I didn't raise you to faint at the sight of blood. Get busy."

Guthrie said, "The females are coming out."

Hareton was too occupied to look. When he did, he saw the yellow eyes peering through the branches.

"They're not as timid as gorillas, either," he said. "Kouram! Take some more men and help quiet those damned animals down!"

Kouram, shouting, ran off to the camels, asses, and goats.

Maranges bent down to observe the skill of the two Ironcastles with needle and gut threads. He said, "Gorillas are *timid?*"

"Generally. All these wild tales you hear about gorillas kidnapping native women and attacking native hunters are just tales. Oh, they do occasionally maul or kill a native, but that's only when they're surprised, caught off guard. And then they usually run. Or try to scare the natives off with a big bluff. I was in Gabon, you know, with an Englishman named Jorkens . . . well, never mind. That's another tale. True, but sounds incredible."

Muriel finished sewing up a scalp gash. She looked across the *boma* and said, "Poor creatures. They're moaning now."

"They'll soon forget," Maranges said. "Apes have short memories."

"But I keep telling you, they're not true apes," Hareton

said. "If I've read my Darwin right, the great apes are distant cousins of ours. Branches of the family tree. But this brute may be one of our forefathers. Descended from our forefathers, I mean. A distant cousin but closer to us than the apes."

"Distant relative!" Maranges said. "I for one do not believe that our ancestor was either a monkey or an ape!"

"Perhaps it's the other way around," Hareton said, grinning. "However, the evidence is overwhelming that we have indeed evolved from some sort of primate. And I suspect that science will uncover an even more overwhelming amount of evidence in the future. At present, it is believed that our hairy Adams and Eves originated in Asia. But, who knows, new evidence may be dug up which will indicate that our ancestors first passed from ape to man on this continent."

Ironcastle continued his sewing and dressing. The ape's chest was now rising and falling slowly. But he remained unconscious.

"If he is to have the slightest chance of survival, he has to be cared for. If we abandon him. . . ."

"We can't do that!" Muriel said.

"No, darling, we won't abandon him. Unless he becomes too great a burden. Or too dangerous to have around."

A man shouted. Hareton looked up and saw Kouram pointing at the north side of the clearing. His hand shook, and he looked ashen under the black skin.

"What is it, Kouram?" Guthrie said.

Kouram moaned, and said, "The Stunted Men."

Hareton, streaked with blood, rose. The clearing seemed deserted. He could see nothing in the darkness beyond. The only sounds were those of some distant beasts.

"I don't see anything," Maranges said.

"The Stunted Men are there," Kouram said. "I saw them."

"What the hell are the Stunted Men?" Hareton said.

"They are men born of the forest. Different from these apes. They are without pity, sly, cunning, impossible to catch. But they can catch men, oh, they can catch men!"

"Over there!" Sir George cried. "See that silhouette in the ferns! There! No, it's gone now!"

"I saw it too," Maranges said. "It did look something like a man."

"A pygmy?" Hareton said.

"No, not a pygmy," Kouram said. "They are not true men, though they have spears, stone axes, and clubs. They are many, they lay traps, they eat. . . ."

He hesitated.

"They eat what?" Guthrie said impatiently.

". . . the fallen, master."

The bonfires growled like living creatures. Now and then, a branch cracked open as if someone out in the bush had stepped on a twig. The sparks rose like fireflies. The forest seemed to breathe, to move a little closer as if it were drawing up to the fire. But it was not like a weary lost traveler grateful for warmth and companionship. It breathed and moved menacingly.

4.

The Stunted Men

"The Stunted Men, the Kwagana," Kouram said, "are born of the Forest, the Swamp and a beast from the clouds."

"Three parents?" Muriel said.

"Yes," Kouram said. "In those days things were not as they are now. Their eyes cast a green light in the night and they can see in the dark. They have large chests and short limbs. Their hair is like the hyena's. They have no nose, just two dark holes above the mouth. They live in tribes, the smallest of which has at least a hundred warriors. They seldom make fire, rarely cook their food, and know nothing of metal-working. Their weapons are wood or stone.

"The Kwagana do not know how to cultivate the land. They are equally ignorant of the art of weaving cloth and making pottery. They eat flesh, nuts, tender shoots, young leaves, roots, and mushrooms. They war among themselves mercilessly. They devour the wounded and the prisoners, men, women, and children. They are especially fond of the flesh of children. The northern tribes, who are red-haired, hate those of the middle country, whose hair is black. Also, those of the west, who are proud of their bluish chests.

"Of recent years, their numbers have been diminishing. They are not at all afraid of death, and they jeer at their torturers. Their faces look as if they were half-man, half-buffalo. They stink like burned flesh."

Maranges said, "How do you know all this? Have you seen the Stunted Men, had intimate contact with them?"

"Yes, shortly after I passed through the initiation rites,

29

became a man, I was taken prisoner by a red-haired tribe.
They planned to eat me, though they did not have to tell
me that. They were laughing because they had other prisoners and some dead. We were tied with lianas while sorcerers were singing in an unknown tongue. They were
holding axes and branches in bloom . . . then we heard
howls from the forest followed by sharp spears. The blue-
chested ones attacked. During the battle, I loosened my
bonds and ran in the direction of the plain."

Now Kouram was quiet, as if dreaming. Hareton was
obviously upset; his main concern was Muriel, or so it
seemed, since he kept looking at her. Maranges was also
gazing at the young girl. But Sydney Guthrie was facing the
darkness without fear or worry. His youth, his vigor, an in-
nate joy, made him careless of the future. Sir George Curtis, after much traveling in the Orient, had contracted some
of the fatalism of the Arabs and Mongols.

"What could these poor devils do to us?" the giant said.
"The machine gun alone is enough to wipe out a tribe. The
elephant gun will tear them to pieces. Maranges and Curtis
are sharpshooters and have guns that fire twenty bullets a
minute. Even Muriel can shoot well. All our men are well-
armed. We can exterminate them at twenty times the distance of a spear throw."

"They know how to make themselves invisible," replied
Kouram. "If a spear strikes men or beasts, it will seem to
come from nowhere."

"The ground around our fires is bare . . . there are
only a few ferns and some grass growing there. . . ."

Something whistled through the night. A shaft, long and
fine, passed over the flames, and they could all see a small
black goat jump. The spear had pierced its flank.

Suddenly, the starlit night had turned from passive menace to active danger. Curtis and Maranges peered into the
darkness. Only the female anthropoids could be seen, their
glowing eyes searching the shadows.

Old Kouram cried out faintly.

"You don't see anything?" Maranges said.

"Master, I can only see that clump of ferns."

Phillippe aimed and shot three times at three different

heights. Two harsh cries were heard; a dark body jumped up, fell, then began to crawl through the low grass. Maranges hesitated before firing at it. Then it disappeared, as if swallowed up by the earth. Long sinister cries, yells akin to the howl of the wolf and the laughter of the hyena, echoed through the clearing and the forest.

The silence was unbroken once more. The Southern Cross marked the eighth hour of the evening. The small black goat bleated, fell down, and died.

Kouram, having extracted the spear, handed it to Ironcastle. The American examined it carefully.

"The point is fashioned from granite. Set up the tents, Kouram."

"Granite!" Sir George said. "How can that be? Are you sure? Here, let me look at it. Granite can't be worked like flint or chert. It has no fracture lines."

Hareton handed it to him. The baronet inspected it carefully, turned it over and over, looked closely through a magnifying glass. Finally, he said, "It *is* granite! 'Strodnary! The edge is as sharp as a worked flint! But how . . . ?"

Hareton said, "We must find out."

"We won't be safe from bullets inside the tents," Hareton said. "But the spears will be slowed down by the canvas."

When the whites were all together in the large tent, the blacks served millet and roasted meat. It was a glum meal; only Guthrie seemed optimistic.

"We'll have to go through the surrounding brush."

"Why?" Maranges said.

"The area around the camp is wide, too far for them to throw their damned weapons. The important thing is to be able to sleep undisturbed."

"But," Hareton said, "going out there would expose us to their spears."

"Why?" Guthrie said. "It isn't necessary."

"Come, come, Sydney. You can't be serious."

"But don't you remember, Uncle Hareton? I expected poisoned arrows. I sent to New York for the necessary armor."

"That's right. You'd told me about that. But I had forgotten."

Guthrie laughed, then yelled, "Hey, Kouram! Bring me the yellow bag!"

Ten minutes later, two Negroes brought a rather flat handbag of light tan leather. They all looked at it with intense curiosity. Sydney opened the case carefully to reveal a pile of garments which looked like rainproof coats.

"A new fabric. As pliable as rubber, yet metallic. Here are the gloves, the masks, the leggings, the hoods."

"You are sure this will withstand arrows?"

"Here."

He unwrapped one of the coats and set it up against the side of the tent. He said to Ironcastle, "Will you throw the spear?"

Hareton took the weapon and hurled it. The spear bounced off the garment.

"The material is intact," Maranges declared. "The granite has only depressed it slightly."

"There was never any doubt," the American said quietly. "Padding and Mortlock furnished the merchandise. They are the best in the world for this type of job. The Stunted Men will waste their poison. Unfortunately, there are also the camels, the asses and the goats. If they should perish, it would do us irreparable harm. That is why I want to cut down any growth around the camp which can hide men."

"A tree trunk and three or four clumps of fern," Sir George said.

Sydney put on the largest garment, fitted a flexible mask over his face, and wrapped the leggings from his ankles to his knees. "Let's settle this matter."

Curtis, Ironcastle, Maranges, Muriel, Kouram and two white servants, Patrick Jefferson and Dick Nightingale, followed suit.

"Let's walk on the side opposite where the animals are," Ironcastle said.

The scarlet moon was climbing up the back of the clearing. Its rays, like a silver ocean, engulfed the ancient forest.

"It's strange that the brutes did not throw another spear," Maranges said.

"The Stunted Men are patient," said Kouram. "They have learned that we have very strong weapons. They will attack us directly only if they are forced to. No matter how well they can hide themselves, there are few places of shelter around the fire. . . ."

"So you think they won't abandon their project?"

"They are more obstinate than the rhinoceros. They will follow us to the end of the forest. Nothing will discourage them. And if we kill any of their warriors, their hatred will grow!"

Curtis, Hareton and Muriel examined every corner of the site with their binoculars.

"Nothing," Hareton said.

"No, nothing," Curtis said. "We can move out." He had taken a long sharp axe which could almost be used as a sickle.

Muriel leaned over the ape. Still in a coma, he looked like a corpse.

"He'll make it," Maranges said, softly.

"Do you think so?" she said. "He has lost so much blood. . . ."

"Only half, at the most. . . ."

A plaintive voice made them turn around. The female anthropoids were still there. The young ones and a mother had fallen asleep.

"They are worried," said Kouram. "They know that the fierce Stunted Men are all around us. They also don't know what we intend to do with the male."

"Won't they attack us?" Ironcastle said.

"I don't think so, master. You did not kill the ape. They know it."

"Let's go," Guthrie said.

The small group went through a narrow space in the enclosure. Guthrie headed toward the nearest clump of ferns and felled it with four strokes of his axe. He cut down the high grass, struck down a short palm tree, and headed for the bush at which Maranges had fired. There was nothing

left in range of a spear cast, no shelter where the Stunted
Men could hide.

"But," Phillippe said, "how could the wounded one have
disappeared?"

"Into a crevice," Kouram answered. Suddenly, he said,
"Here he is."

In two short leaps Guthrie, Maranges, and Curtis joined
him. They saw a man stretched out in a crevice, completely
unmoving. Hair as red as that of the fox covered his head
and spotted his cheeks. His head was like a square, cut off
at the jaw, and he seemed neckless. His complexion was
the color of turf, his arms were flattened and ended in extraordinarily short hands, like the pincers of crabs. The
short feet had broad short toes covered with a hornlike
substance. The shoulders were broad and his chest was
deep.

He was almost naked. Blood was coagulating on his bel-
ly and on his chest. He wore a belt made of rawhide. A
green axe, a stone knife, and two spears lay in the crevice
by him.

"The three bullets hit him," Kouram said. "But he's not
dead. Should I finish him?"

"Don't you dare!" Maranges cried, horrified.

"He's a hostage," Guthrie said coldly.

He bent down and rose with the Stunted Man in his
arms as he would have done with a child. At this, someone
growled, and six or seven spears whistled forth, two of
which hit Kouram and Guthrie. The giant began to laugh,
while Kouram, with many gestures, indicated to the invisible enemy that their attack was in vain.

Curtis' sharp eyes were scrutinizing the forest. Approximately fifty meters away he could see a bush large enough
to hide two or three men.

"What should we do?" Sir George asked.

"We must make them fear us. If they attack, we coun-
terattack. Fire at will!"

They all raised their rifles but Guthrie said, "Hold it!
Pardon me, Uncle Hareton, shouldn't we try to take some
prisoners? If we can question them, we might find out
something about them and about this country."

Hareton frowned, then he said, "You are right, of course."

Guthrie tossed his elephant rifle to his gun-bearer. He removed a .38 Husquevarna revolver from his holster. Holding it in both hands, he pointed it at the bush. "The elephant gun would blow a man apart," he said. "At this range, the .38 might just wound enough to incapacitate. We'll see."

He squeezed the trigger. Immediately following the report, a cry came from behind the bush. A figure stood up, swayed, then collapsed sideways.

"Poor beast!" Phillippe said.

"Let's not waste our pity," Sydney said. "The poor beasts are killers by vocation and cannibals by principle. There is no other way to teach them to fear our strength."

He grabbed the unconscious creature and held him under his arm as he headed back toward the camp. The white servants had by then removed all possible hiding places that Maranges and Guthrie hadn't taken care of. For a hundred meters around, no one could hide himself, no matter how crafty he might be.

Sydney set down the Stunted Man close to the ape. Hareton began to dress his wounds. Two or three times, without coming to, the wounded man gave a plaintive cry.

"He is less badly wounded than the anthropoid."

Kouram was looking at the Stunted Man with hate and apprehension. "It would be best to kill him," he said. "We will have to watch him all the time."

"We have ropes," Guthrie said. He lit his pipe. "The night will be quiet. Tomorrow we'll have daylight."

Muriel removed her mask and her metallic garment. Now she was dreaming, looking up at Orion, a constellation of her homeland, and the Southern Cross, which symbolized the unknown land. Phillippe was rapt, charmed. She seemed like a mountain nymph rising in the forest dawn, like a water sprite from a lake in the twilight. Phillippe grew pale at the thought of the peril which menaced her.

"Can't we do anything for those poor beasts?" she said, indicating the female anthropoids.

"They don't need us," he said, smiling. "The whole forest is their realm. They can find in abundance all they need to be happy."

"But, you see . . . they're not leaving. They must be afraid of the red Stunted Men. But they haven't been attacked by them, have they?"

"They did not attack them," he said, "because they must be saving their weapons for us."

"For us," she said with a sigh and turned her head toward Ironcastle. He was finishing up dressing the wounds of the Stunted Man.

His heart full of a sad sweetness, all at once Phillippe savored stellar space, the shining ashes which settled down over the underbrush and this supple daughter of America, who looked like the daughters of the island where pagan Angels lived whose beauty charmed Saint Gregory. Maranges was a warrior, but he was singularly romantic for a Frenchman, who are supposed to be so coldly practical.

5.

The Waterhole

Hareton took the last watch of the night. Three blacks stood guard with him, all watching the clearing periphery.

A night just like all the nights in the forest, a night of ambush and murder, of triumphs and misery, a hurricane of screaming, roaring, howling, bellowing, throat rattles and cries of agony, of flesh devoured alive, of swallowing bellies and bellies being eaten, anguish, fear, ferocity, lust. The feast of some and the horror of others, death satiating life. . . .

"Each night, for millions of years," thought Hareton. "Each night without leave and without pity . . . each night, harmless beasts, which have had so much trouble to survive, have perished due to an inconceivable necessity . . . and will perish! Lord! How Thy will is mysterious."

The white glow of the sky weighed lightly on the dark spaces of the forest. Smells floated around—fresh as springs, exquisite as music, intoxicating as young women, wild as lions, ambiguous as reptiles. . . .

A heavy melancholy lay upon the American. Full of regret for having brought Muriel along, he could not understand his own weakness.

"One must believe," he told himself, "that each man has, not only his hour, but his season of madness."

She had never left him. She was the last of his children, Hareton having lost his two sons when the *Thunder* was torpedoed just off the coast of Spain. Ever since, he had been unable to resist the wishes of his daughter.

Toward dawn, a fog appeared, making all things look less sharp. The veiled light of the moon deformed the

37

shape of the trees. The stars covered themselves with a pale shroud, through which they twinkled like weak watch lights.

In his imagination, Ironcastle saw Muriel carried away by the Stunted Men, and terrible visions tormented him.

Three jackals trotted into the clearing, stopped, and looked at the fire. Hareton looked at them, thought of his own dogs, and was homesick. Then they ran away in the underbrush, and vast silence covered all things once more.

"And yet, the enemy is there," Hareton thought.

In spite of his uneasiness, Hareton was under the vast spell of this silence broken by the light sounds of crackling flames, of the shivering passage of beasts, of the sigh of leaves.

A lighter fog rose toward the stars, the unfathomable fog of dawn, the dew sputtering as it hit the bonfires. The three blacks roamed around as the dawn brightened, the dawn which seemed to come as much from the trees as the heavens. The dreadful visions of the awakening day floated away in an instant. And then the day was there. In the unknown and unknowable depths, millions of timid beasts rose. Hareton drew from his pocket a small Bible.

Hareton read, then joining his hands, he prayed. His life was divided into two distinct compartments. In one was his Faith to Science; in the other, his Faith in Divine Revelation.

"There we are," he told himself. "All we have to do is to protect the animals. I could have saved the goat by cauterizing it. . . ."

A shadow passed close to him. Before turning his head, he knew that it was Muriel.

"Darling," he whispered, "I was wrong to bend to your will."

"Are you so sure," she replied, "that we wouldn't come across greater danger without leaving our country? Who knows," she said, "what's going on in America?"

Jovial laughter interrupted her. The giant Guthrie suddenly appeared before the dying flames.

"What could be going on that isn't a repetition of what was happening before we left? I suppose that thousands of ships are filling the harbors of the United States . . . that

railroads are carrying city dwellers who are leaving the
beaches to return home . . . that factories are roaring . . .
farmers thinking of the fall harvest . . . the good people
are taking their evening meal. Over there, night is falling,
the buses, the streetcars, and the automobiles are filling the
streets of Baltimore. . . ."

"No doubt," Phillippe said, gravely. "But there could
also have been some great cataclysms there."

"An earthquake?" Curtis said.

"Why not? Is there any reason for England and France
to be forever free from the danger of earthquakes? Anyway, the United States has experienced them. But I was
thinking of something else. . . ."

The light of the coming day, which seemed like the light
of creation, was taking hold of the forest. The last flames
were out. Wings dazzled the upper reaches of the forest.

"Let's have breakfast," Sydney said. "Then we'll hold a
council of war."

Kouram gave some orders. Two blacks brought tea, coffee, canned goods, preserves, biscuits, smoked buffalo, and
sausages. Guthrie ate breakfast with that joyful energy
which he always brought to a meal.

"How is the gorilla?" he said to Kouram.

"Still unconscious, master, but the Stunted Man is awakening."

Phillippe was serving Muriel. The young girl, while
munching some biscuits and drinking tea, was contemplating the site.

"They are still there," she said softly.

She was pointing to the group of anthropoids who had
slept close to the fires.

"That's strange," Phillippe said. "I think that Kouram is
right. They are afraid of the Stunted Men, although they
must not be thinking of the apes while they are watching
enemies like us."

Muriel's great turquoise eyes became dreamlike, and
Phillippe said to himself softly, "And how they will dread
the passing of their days, those who spend them close to
her!"

Guthrie, having finished his smoked buffalo and his coffee, said, "Now, let's make plans. As long as we are in the clearing, we'll be safe from the Stunted Men. To attack us, they must come out into the open. But we can't stay in the clearing without water and without firewood. Water is a mile away. And we can't do without wood."

"What can we gain by making camp here?" Maranges asked.

"That will let us make the less vulnerable blacks who cannot be protected by the metallic garments," Ironcastle said. "We also must protect our animals. If we lost them, it would be disastrous."

"What if these damned cannibals get reinforcements?" Hareton said anxiously, "Karoum, can they?"

"It is possible, master. But the red ones rarely make allies unless it is against the blue chests. Their tribes live far apart from one another."

"So," Phillippe said, "chances are even better that our besiegers could meet friends along the march."

"So we camp?" Sydney said. He didn't seem to care one way or another.

"That's my opinion," Ironcastle said.

"And mine," added Sir George quietly.

"How's the water supply, Kouram?"

"We don't have enough for the animals. We were counting on the waterhole."

"We must make a sortie!"

Beyond the enclosure of ashes and the empty zone, there was nothing but pale islets of fern, grass, or shrubs. Beyond that, the mysterious country of the trees.

"The camp must be well guarded," Guthrie said. "Uncle Hareton, you are the most expert with the machine gun. You'll have to stay with Muriel, Patrick Jefferson, and most of the blacks. Curtis, Maranges, Kouram, Dick Nightingale, two blacks and myself will make a sortie as far as the waterhole. Too bad we won't be able to bring a camel."

Ironcastle shook his head. He didn't like the idea of a sortie. "We could wait awhile longer."

"No. If we wait, the risk will be greater. We must decide now."

"Sydney's right," Phillippe said.

Those who were to go on the sortie put on the metallic garments and masks. Guthrie had his elephant gun, an axe and two revolvers. Maranges and Curtis had identical equipment, except for the rifle. Dick Nightingale also carried a heavy dirk.

"Let's go!"

The words were like the clang of a tocsin. A faint trembling shook the shoulders of the young girl. The forest suddenly seemed more ferocious and enormous.

Three blacks formed a wide-based triangle. Phillippe, whose hearing was extraordinary, followed Kouram. Sydney took very long steps, his great strength even more reassuring the blacks than the elephant gun or the carbines of Curtis and Maranges, though they seldom missed. The others formed a rear guard.

They headed east. A honey badger ran under the palm trees, and some antelopes fled rapidly. At the end of the clearing Kouram, moving slowly, probed the dark green patches with his spear.

"Be careful," Phillippe said.

Among the creaking sounds, the furtive slitherings, and the almost imperceptible noise that seemed to be the breath of the forest, he thought he discerned some sort of organized movement.

They found some beaten paths, ancient ways where beasts and perhaps men made their wary approach to the waterhole. The small troop had drawn in upon itself, Kouram still leading, followed closely by the two blacks.

"Perhaps they've fled," Guthrie whispered.

"I've heard too many bodies sliding among the plants," Maranges answered.

"You have the ear of a wolf."

Kouram called for a halt. One of the blacks spread himself on the ground.

"Someone's walking over there," Phillippe said, indicating some dense growths on the right side of a baobab.

"It's them," Kouram said. "But they are also ahead of us. And to the left. They're all around us. They know we're going to the waterhole."

The invisible presence was nerve-wracking. They were

caught in a yielding trap, shifting yet solid, a moving trap that disappeared to strike more effectively.

In the greenish light, a silver glittering revealed the presence of water, mother of all beings. When they got closer, they saw a small lake. Giant white water lilies spread their petals; a large number of birds rose with a long sighing sound; a nervous dik-dik stopped drinking.

The expedition stopped next at a promontory where plants had been torn out by elephants, rhinocerosi, buffaloes, and antelopes. Clear and almost fresh, the water must have been fed by an underground current; it left the lake by three rivulets.

The blacks drank avidly. Afraid of water pollution, the whites, having filled their canteens, poured into them several drops of a yellowish liquid.

"Now for the water bags."

Suddenly, a clamor exploded, fantastic and horrifying, seeming almost rhythmic. Two howls followed by a throat rattle. Human forms sprang up and disappeared. Then, silence fell, as penetrating as the silence preceding a storm.

"It sounds like many many men," Kouram murmured.

The faces of the blacks became ashen. They were brave men, but their fear of the unnatural and the supernatural chilled them to their innermost beings. Curtis and Maranges kept their eyes on the underbrush. Guthrie raised his elephant gun.

Spears flew from the brush, but they hit the metallic garments without doing any harm or fell into the lake.

"Without the armor, we would have all perished," Sydney said cheerfully.

"These spears can be useful," Sir George said, as he picked up one that had bounced from his chest. "They are more dangerous to them than they are to us."

"Yes, those no-good worms are supplying us with weapons."

The water bags had been dropped on the promontory. The small troop awaited, spread out in a half circle, the lake behind them. All the animals had fled; the only sign of life was a strange bird flying over the water.

"What are they waiting for?" Guthrie said with a trace of impatience.

"They want to see if we will die," Kouram answered. "The poison on the speartips is slow . . . but sure."

Only the faraway cry of a monkey could be heard on the other side of the lake. The silence seemed endless. Then, the clamor began once more, and two bands of Stunted Men charged. There were at least sixty, smeared with crimson and armed with stakes, clubs or stone axes.

"Fire!" Curtis yelled.

He and Maranges, each shooting twice, had put four men out of the fight when the voice of the elephant gun resounded. The effect was monstrous: arms and legs flew apart, a head hung by its hair from the limbs of a baobab; entrails slithered like blue snakes. Howling with fear, the Stunted Men beat a hasty retreat and vanished, except for one troop which rose from the reeds and fell savagely on the party. A blow from a club felled Kouram. Assailed by two Stunted Men, one of the blacks fell. Two Stunted Men appeared in front of Phillippe. Their faces were stained crimson; their eyes were phosphorescent; their short massive arms brandished green axes.

Maranges, warding off the blows with his rifle, laid one attacker on the ground. The second one, attacking from the side, brought down his weapon. But Phillippe managed to duck. Carried away by his thrust, the Stunted Man went as far as the shore. Then Maranges kicked him into the lake.

Guthrie was holding his own against three Stunted Men. They were hesitant, scared by his giant size. Sydney knocked aside a club, grabbed a creature by the neck, whirled him around like a club, and threw him at his comrades, bowling them over. Sir George, running up to help, knocked out the heaviest of the aggressors with a blow from his rifle stock.

It became a rout. The unhurt men fled into the shelter of the reeds. Those that were wounded crawled toward the forest. As had been agreed, Guthrie blew three blasts from his whistle, one long and two short, to let Ironcastle know that the danger had passed.

"We must take prisoners," Curtis said, grabbing a bleeding half-stunned man.

Guthrie and Dick did likewise. Four wounded men now were in the hands of the victors.

"Where is Kouram?" Maranges said anxiously.

Kouram answered with a sigh, followed by a grunt. The thickness of his hair and the strength of his skull had preserved him. The second black was standing up. He seemed to have a dislocated shoulder.

Twenty minutes later, the expedition was on its way back to the camp. It was formed into a square, at the center of which the captives dragged themselves. Twice, the war cry of the Stunted Men rose from the forest, but no attack was made.

When he'd heard gunfire Ironcastle, ready for battle, had the machine gun brought forward. The signals from Guthrie reassured him. During the interval that followed, his worry grew anew. He was on the point of making a sortie when the expedition came into view at the eastern end of the clearing. The caravan was moving slowly, held up by the captives.

"No losses?" Hareton yelled when Phillippe and Guthrie were close enough.

"None. One of the blacks hurt his shoulder, that's all."

"Were there many of them?" Muriel asked.

Guthrie said, "About sixty attacked from the front. Ten came at us from the reeds. If that's the whole tribe, our worries are over."

"That's not the whole tribe," Kouram said.

"He's right," Phillippe said. "There were many voices coming from the rear. The attack having failed, the reserves did not show themselves."

"How many warriors do you think there are?" Hareton asked Kouram.

"At least ten times the fingers of the hand and five times more."

"A hundred and fifty. They could storm the camp."

"They will not try," Kouram said. "And they will not attack in a large group again until they catch us in a trap.

Now they know your weapons. They know that their spears are useless against the yellow coats."

"You don't think they'll give up trying to surround us?"

"They are all around us just as light fills the whole forest."

Ironcastle lowered his head. "We cannot organize our departure in a single day." Manifestly worried about Muriel, he kept glancing at her.

"That is certain," Maranges said. He shared the same worry.

"And we need water and food for ourselves and the animals."

"I don't think they'll attack us again on the road to the waterhole," Sydney said.

"No, master," Kouram said. "They will attack us neither today nor tomorrow. They are waiting for the moment we leave. The animals will be able to eat while under the protection of our guns."

The entire group suddenly felt the pressure of the formidable unknown. Between them and their homeland lay the forest, the desert, the ocean. And, very close, a strange enemy, both man and beast. This enemy, poorly armed, had the strength of numbers on his side, as well as cunning and stubbornness. In spite of their rifles, their machine gun, their armored suits, the travelers were highly vulnerable.

"How are the wounded?" Maranges said.

Hareton pointed to a small tent. "There they are. The man has regained consciousness, but he is extremely weak. The ape is still drowsy."

Of the rest of the captives, none was seriously hurt.

"I find them uglier than the apes," Guthrie said. "There is something of the hyena and the rhinoceros about them. Those brutal painted faces, those glaring eyes . . . alien . . . unnatural."

"It is not so much their ugliness that strikes me as their expression," Hareton said. "It's a human expression, but it shows the worst in humanity. It reveals, to an extreme degree, that defect which is found only in men and apes."

"What about panthers and tigers?" Muriel said.

"They are naively ferocious," retorted Hareton. "They

are not evil. There is in human wickedness a sort of tran-
scendency unknown in the worst carnivores. Judging by
their appearance, these Stunted Men are among the most
wicked segments of humanity."

"It's a sort of superiority," Curtis growled.

Kouram, who had been listening without really under-
standing, said passionately, "Don't keep any captives!
More dangerous than snakes . . . they will signal other
Stunted Men. Why don't you cut off their heads?"

6.

The Worm and the Wild Boar

For three days, the travelers worked to get ready for their departure. An antelope having been caught by the blacks, Ironcastle made some experiments on it with the poisoned spears. Immediate cauterizing neutralized the effect of the poison.

"Good!" said Guthrie. "Now we must try this on one of the captives."

"We don't have the right to do that," his uncle said.

"To me, it's a duty," retorted his nephew. "To hesitate between the life of one of these brave men and that of one of these scoundrels is pure folly!"

Arming himself with a spear, he grabbed one of the captives who was being held in one of the tents. He was the most stunted of the band; his width was half his height. His round eyes gazed upon the giant with a ferocity in which there was, however, a glint of fear. After a slight hesitation Sydney jabbed the man in the shoulder. The man stiffened, but his face expressed both disdain and hatred.

"There you are, Uncle Hareton, I will carry the sin myself alone. You be the good healer!"

Ironcastle quickly cauterized the wound. After half an hour, no sign of poisoning had manifested itself.

"You see how right I was," Guthrie said. "Cauterization can save men as well as animals."

As Kouram had foreseen, no new attack occurred.

Each morning, an expedition went as far as the lake. Two camels were brought along, covered with heavy linen, the same linen that had been meant for tent repairs. The blacks carried back fodder to add to the grass and tender

47

growths the camels, asses and goats were eating in the clearing.

The Stunted Men did not appear.

"You would almost believe they've gone away," Maranges said on the evening of the fourth day. They had long been listening to the faint undefinable noises of the forest.

"They will only go away if we force them to do so," Kouram said. "They are all around us, but far enough away so that we can't hear or smell them."

The captives were scarcely feeling their wounds now, except for the one picked up the first night. All of them kept a distant look on their faces and listened constantly. They did not respond to the signs by which Ironcastle or his companions tried to make themselves understood.

Their faces, as unmoving as stone masks, seemed as stupid as those of rhinoceri or hippopotami. However, two emotions slowly manifested themselves. When they spotted Guthrie, their eyes dilated ferociously. When seeing Muriel, the same eyes shone with an obscure undecipherable light.

"It's with your help, both of you, that we can begin to attempt taming them," Hareton said.

Those words made Maranges uneasy. In the brutish eyes, something untamable, malicious, seemed to lurk. The others did not see this, but he was more sensitive than they.

Another event interested the travelers. The ape had regained consciousness. He was extremely weak, shaking with fever. When he became aware of the men around him, at first he seemed afraid. His eyelids trembled and he attempted to raise his head, but feeling too weak, he resigned himself. Since no one was hurting him, and since repetition influences a beast even more than man, he adjusted to his surroundings. Except for a few recurrences of aversion or fear, he accepted peacefully the visits of the explorers. He even showed an attachment to Ironcastle, who fed and took care of him.

"He is certainly less unmanageable than these stunted brutes," the naturalist said. "We will tame him."

The expedition once more moved on its way.

Although tangly, the forest was not impossible. The

trees, often monstrous, especially the baobabs and the date trees, rarely formed themselves into clusters. The lianas were not abundant, nor were the thorn bushes or the shrubs.

"This forest is comfortable," remarked Guthrie, who was walking ahead of the group along with Sir George and Kouram. "I wonder why we have come across so few human beings."

"Not so few," retorted Curtis. "In the first region we counted at least three types of blacks, which supposes a relatively large number of clans. And we are being pursued by the Stunted Men, who are far from few."

"It is they who are keeping other men from living farther on," Kouram remarked.

Curtis and Guthrie had few characteristics in common, though they were both of Anglo-Saxon origin, mixed with Celt in the American's case. Sir George's mind was as concentrated as that of Ironcastle while Sydney's scattered itself in waves. In times of danger, Curtis fell back upon himself, to the point of seeming indifferent or plunged into a dream. All his emotions were then buried, hiding in the fog of unconsciousness. There was nothing in the foreground but the vigilance of his senses and the workings of purely objective thought.

On the other hand, peril excited Guthrie violently. During combat he was seized by a cheerful madness which did not keep him from retaining control over his decisions and movements.

In short, Curtis' bravery was solemn and Guthrie's was joyful. Their opinions differed as much as their character. Sydney mixed spiritualism and the occult with his faith. Sir George conformed to the rites of the English church which he accepted in full. Each tolerated a diversity of sects as long as the fundamental prescriptions of the Gospels were respected.

Two days went by without any adventures. In the silent and closed-in forest, only a few furtive beasts fled before the caravan. Even the birds were silent, except for a few that raised their strident voices intermittently. Curtis and Guth-

rie believed that the Stunted Men had remained behind.
Even Kouram began to doubt that they were present.

In the early afternoon, the trees became sparse, and the
group found itself in a sort of savanna, where wooded islets
alternated with grassy areas and deserted strands.

The territory consisted of two very distinct regions. To
the east, the savanna predominated, while to the west the
forest continued, though broken by clearings. The explorers remained on the border between the two regions to en-
sure themselves of the advantages of both.

A swamp, going beyond the edge of the forest, en-
croached upon the savanna. It was bordered by tall papyri,
the leaves of which trembled in the feeble breeze that was
forever aborning and dying. It was a land of reptiles, moist,
chaotic, full of crevices and rifts. Giant white water lilies
spread leaves which resembled cups, enveloped with algae
on which fed beasts from the deep, while birds of many
hues made the air clang.

"We'll stop for lunch and for a rest," Hareton said.

While the blacks were settling the caravan under the
baobabs, Muriel, Sir George, Sydney, and Phillippe explored the shore of the lake. Muriel stopped close to a
creek. Everywhere were heavenly flowers, immense butter-
flies all fire and jonquil and scarlet, green or turquoise flies
dancing lightly. A frog as large as a rat jumped into the
torpid waters. Limp forms appeared, a large mouth
emerged from the water, black fish fled rapidly, testifying
to a monstrous life below. An almost fabled apparition
drew Muriel from her contemplation. More than any other
creature in the ageless forest, it brought to mind dark
forces and a frightful chaos. A thick larva, long as a tree
trunk, covered with a multi-hued shell, it was crawling with
a repulsive agility, guided by a small head with beady eyes.
All that is hideous in an earthworm, a leech, or a slug manifested itself in a colossal way. No one could say if it saw
the young girl; its eyes were like an opaque mineral.

A wild disgust froze Muriel's flesh. It was unclean, like a
beast come from the nether regions. Her terror was even
deeper, her revulsion more awful than when the lions had
entered the clearing. Muriel's trembling legs hit a stump;

she tripped, fell to her knees. Excited by the fall, the thing crawled rapidly and coiled its vast body around that of the young girl. She tried to scream but horror choked her. The worm's head was poised in front of the frozen chalklike face. The coils of the giant were choking off her breath and cracking her vertebrae. Her mind sank into darkness. . . .

Sir George and Phillippe were walking together along the shore of the swamp. The water, the reeds, the grasses, and the shrubs were thick. Each seemed to vibrate slightly. Of course, this was their imagination.

"This place is blessed with a terrifying fecundity," Sir George said. "Especially the insects. . . ."

"Insects are the abomination of the world," Phillippe said. "Just look at these flies. There's not one spot that they don't grab. There they are, ready to eat and to destroy anything in sight. Sir George, insects will destroy us."

Sir George, who stood in the midst of a clump of papyrus, suddenly shouted hoarsely, "My God, look at that!"

Phillippe looked where he was pointing, and he too cried out. Up on the promontory, the worm was on the point of completely enveloping Muriel. The glittering head was resting on her shoulder and a horrible aura seemed to emanate from both.

Phillippe had reached for his carbine, but Sir George shouted, "The revolver and the knife!"

They leaped forward and quickly climbed to the promontory. They could not tell whether or not the beast had noticed their presence. It was undulating, it was shuddering, concentrating upon its horrible work. Simultaneously, Sir George and Phillippe riddled the head with shots from their revolvers and they began to cut the huge body to pieces. The coils gave way and uncurled. Phillippe had grabbed the young girl and was laying her down on the ground. Already she was coming to, a wild look on her nymphlike face.

"Don't say a word to my father, you mustn't!"

"We shan't say a word," Sir George said.

She rose and laughed briefly, though her laughter had no mirth in it.

"That kind of death is unclean. You've doubly saved my life." And she turned away shuddering.

Guthrie had followed the shore of the swamp. He was admiring this fearsome creation which, without end, kept converting minerals into living matter. This vast area of dirty water was feeding a multitude of plants and one could imagine the fabulous animal life that moved around in the depths.

He had reached a fantastic bay, full of muddy nooks, of vegetable flesh and dry ground where twenty herds could have found refuge. A hundred yards from where he stood was a fantastic animal, a sort of boar, tall, with a colossal head. It had a swollen face, full of warts, its snout armed with curved tusks, thick, sharp and prominent, a smooth skin, with hair on its back and a long mane.

"By Old Nick, it's a wild boar," the young man thought. "And damnedly beautiful, in its own way. . . ."

The beast grunted again and eyed Guthrie. It would flee only when facing a rhinoceros, an elephant, or a lion. Even then, unable to escape, it would have accepted combat. During the dark millennia, how often had the lion succumbed to his curved tusks . . . but, however ready to meet battle, the boar does not seek it. Only during the time of folly, the savage and ferocious enchantment of the mating season, or when fear transforms into fury, or it is necessary to fight its way through a trap, does it attack.

This one was grunting because it expected an attack. Between dense growths its small eyes shone above the wart-covered cheeks.

"We don't have much in the way of provisions," Guthrie said to himself.

He hesitated, however, feeling indulgent toward the mighty beast. This one, a male in the prime of life, bore in its loins the seed of a thousand other boars as mighty as it was. And Guthrie, just like Theodore Roosevelt, did not want to rid the world of mighty animals which recalled the prehistory of man. As he was meditating, a second boar trotted from the swamp and immediately afterward, ten young ones, both awful and superb. Suddenly, taking off at a run, they seemed to charge right at Guthrie. He threw

"They seemed to charge right at Guthrie."

himself to the left while the horde went on, but the big
male which he had first seen was charging blindly. Guthrie
had no time to draw or aim. The long tusks were trying to
tear him apart when, with a blow of his fist, he struck the
beast behind the ear. It retreated, squealing. Its eyes
seemed to flame. Sydney was laughing, a laugh both joyful
and barbaric, proud of having stopped the mighty beast in
its tracks. He yelled for his adversary to resume its attack.

The boar came on again, and the Yankee leaped to the
left. Then his fists came down like a hammer on the neck,
in the ribs, and on the snout. The animal was running
around in circles, shifting in mid-stride, charging and snorting. The antagonists found themselves on the edge of a
moat. Grabbing the boar by a leg and shoving it on the
shoulder, Sydney threw it in the mud. The animal struggled
in the mire to the other shore, while Sydney shouted like a
triumphant Hercules.

"I've decided to spare you, monster of the swamp!"

7.

The Wild Cavern

The forest plants became more numerous; the trees, more abundant and with denser foliage; the shrubs, thicker. Progress became even more difficult. The group was forced to fall back on the savanna. It was comprised of red dirt and exotic plants, alternating with rocky surfaces. Purple serpents slithered into holes. Blue lizards warmed themselves on rocks. Here and there, an ostrich ran in the solitude. Then, only rocks and lichen could be seen, the latter eating away at the stone for countless centuries. Finally, a chain of hills rose in teethlike crests.

Guthrie, having climbed a hill, cried out with enthusiasm. Lost among three ageless solitudes, the forest, the savanna and the desert, a lake spread its inexhaustible waters.

The forest, filling the east with its nations of trees, was separated from the savanna by red rocks and dead sands, on which even the lichen was dying, and beyond the brush the savanna was in charge of the west.

Because of this conjunction of various territories, the lake welcomed on its shores all the strange beasts of the desert, the cunning beasts of the prairie, the numberless hosts of the trees. There were the ostrich, the baroque boar, the monstrous rhinoceros, the hippopotamus, the lion, the leopard, the jackal, the hyena, the antelope, the zebra and the dromedary, the great ape, the baboon, the elephant and the buffalo, the python and the crocodile. Eagles and vultures, storks, ibis, cranes, flamingos, herons, kingfishers. . . .

"An admirable solitude," Guthrie said. "For how many

thousands of years has this lake supported the immense life which man will have destroyed or subdued before the end of the twentieth century?"

"Do you think they will destroy it?" Curtis asked.

Guthrie burst out laughing. "I predict that the factories of Europe and America will send their smoke floating above all the savannas and that they will consume all the forests. However, if it should turn out otherwise, I would not shed tears. I would accept the return of the beasts."

A band of wild asses, full of untamed grace, and some odd-looking gnus jumped on a promontory. Three tall ostriches advanced on a sterile beach, guided by their instinctual need for wide-open spaces. Some buffaloes also came forth, a band of baboons, an old rhino protected by his natural armor, heavy, sluggish yet formidable, feared even by lions. Then, fearful, though standing above all beings with their long necks, a few giraffes ran by.

"What an enigma," Sir George growled. "Why all these strange forms? Why the ugliness of this rhinoceros and the absurd head of this ostrich?"

"All are beautiful when compared with this one," Guthrie said, pointing toward a huge hippo. "What can the monstrous jaws, the ugly eyes, of this giant pig's body signify?"

"You can be sure, Sydney, that this all makes wonderful sense."

"I'll go along with that," the giant said, carelessly. "Where will we make camp?"

As they were looking around, colossal beasts moved out of the forest. They were walking forward gravely, formidable yet peaceful. Their legs seemed like tree trunks, their bodies like rocks, their skin like movable bark. Their trunks moved before them like pythons and their tusks looked like great curved picks. The earth trembled. Buffaloes, boars, antelopes, and zebras made way before the monstrous horde. Two lions headed for the trees, while the giraffes raised their heads anxiously.

"Don't you think that the elephants bring to mind giant insects?" Guthrie said.

"That is certainly true," retorted Sir George. "I compare

them to dung beetles and other insects. There must be females among them that weigh ten thousand pounds, Sydney.
It's a glorious spectacle."

The immense herd was invading the lake. The trumpet-
ings seemed to shake the air. The mothers watched their
young, which were as tall as wild asses, as playful as young
dogs.

"If mankind was not around," Curtis said dreamily,
"nothing would be as mighty on the face of the Earth. And
that might would not be evil."

"All would not recognize that strength. You see that rhino, over there, on the promontory. It wouldn't back off if
it had to face the mightiest of these lords. Hey, let's not
forget about the camp!"

"I can see, over there close to the forest, but still in the
savanna, a bare spot between three rocks, neither too close
nor too far from the lake."

Sir George pointed with his right hand while he held his
binoculars with his left. "It will be easy to maintain a fire
over there."

Guthrie examined the emplacement and found it good.

"However," he said after a few moments, "I would also
like that other spot, dug out of the brush, which forms a
half circle. If it's okay with you, one of us will explore it,
while the other will go as far as the Three Rocks."

"Wouldn't it be best to stick together?"

"I think that we'll both bring back information enough
to make a decision. Seen from here, both spots seem equally worthwhile. If we find that both places are even, we'll
toss a coin to decide. Let's save some time."

"I'm not so sure that we *will* save time but we probably
won't lose any. Let's go. Even though I don't like to split
up."

"For less than an hour."

"Very well! And you pick . . . ?"

"I'll head for the Three Rocks."

Although Guthrie was walking rapidly, followed by
Kouram and another black, he took almost half an hour to
reach the edge of the forest. He found the spot even more
spacious and comfortable than he had anticipated. Two of

the rocks were bare, and their sides were red. A third, by
far the largest, was full of lumps and hollows. Some banyan
trees were growing in a hollow. A dark hole was the entrance to a cavern.

"Kouram," the giant said, "you examine the terrain from
here to the pointed rock. Your comrade will do the same
from here to the round rock. We'll meet back here."

"Be careful of the cavern, master," Kouram said.

Guthrie headed for the hollowed rock. Its shape was sur-
prisingly architectural. A notched tower, a truncated pyra-
mid, suggestions of obelisks, arches, ovals, vague pedi-
ments, gothic needles, everywhere the untiring labor of
lichens, pellitories, wind, and sand.

This wild place could become hospitable. The cavern
and the great hollows could, with some alterations, be
made fool-proof against wild animals and a fortress against
men.

"This is where we should make camp," he thought.

Kouram's words came back to him. "Beware of the cavern."

Guthrie mixed temerity and foresight in variable doses,
sometimes as thoughtful as Ironcastle himself, yet more
daring. He was wont to give way suddenly to the madness
of adventure.

This wild release of his enormous energy kept him from
using it against himself. His experiences all over the world
had given him excessive self-confidence. When he was box-
ing, no amateur could resist him; he would have been a
match for Dempsey. He could hold up a horse and its rider. His ability to high jump and long jump was amazing,
considering his one hundred and four kilograms weight.

The cavern was even vaster than he had imagined.
Membranous wings brushed against him. A night bird
opened phosphorescent eyes in the darkness. Crawling
beasts wound their way around on the ground. Finally, he
was forced to light the electric lamp.

The Yankee saw a swarm of underground beasts fleeing
from the light into fissures. An irregular vault was covered
with bats, many of which detached themselves and flew in

circles, emitting sharp cries, rising and falling on their silent wings.

Many galleries appeared, and at the other end of the cavern, two holes shone with a faint, uncertain glimmer. He walked through one of these holes, which rapidly became too small for him to proceed. Then, by the rays of the lamp, Guthrie saw a rousing spectacle. At the end of the fissure, in the lateral partition, two holes with cutting edges, one sloping to the left and the other to the right, opened onto other caves. They must have opened on the western wall of the rock, which Guthrie had yet to see. A dim light penetrated the holes where the light of the lamp traced purplish cones. In the cave on the right, three male lions and two females stood frightened by the intruding light. Their young cubs stretched themselves in the shadows. The males were as giant as the vanished lions of the Atlas Mountains, the females reminiscent of blonde tigresses.

"Life is magnificent," the giant thought.

He began to laugh passionately. These fearful beasts were at his mercy. Two or three shots from his elephant gun, and the savage kings would enter eternal night. The ancient soul of the hunter rose in him. He aimed his rifle. Doubt and caution took hold of him and then, turning his head, he began to shake.

From a second cave still more formidable dwellers had emerged. In none of the many American circus menageries had Sydney ever seen lions comparable to those that stood in the dim light. They seemed to have suddenly appeared from the far reaches of prehistory, giants resembling the tiger-lion, the *felis spelaea* of ancient caverns. . . .

Thunder bounced off the red granite. All the lions were roaring together. Guthrie was awed, yet somehow pleased. Once more he aimed his gun but, shaking his head and giving way to unutterable feelings, he retreated. "We won't set up camp here," he thought.

Once he found himself out in the open again, he headed rapidly toward Kouram and the other black. They were walking in the direction of the rocks, and he signaled them to go no farther. They waited for the giant who was

"The cave lion."

hurrying because, at any moment, the lions might come out of their lair.

A roar split the wide expanse. A lion had just bounded forth, followed by a lioness. They were not the immense beasts of the second cave but their size still surprised Kouram. They did not, however, seem aggressive. The time had not yet come for these sovereigns of the animal kingdom to demonstrate why they ruled. However, just to be on the safe side, Sydney cocked his gun and checked the free movement of the Bowie in its sheath. He had six cartridges in his revolver. . . .

Another deeper and louder roar sounded. One of the colossal lions was emerging from the shadow of the rocks.

"Damnit," Guthrie growled, "we're playing heads or tails with death."

The first lion charged. In six leaps, he traveled half the distance that separated him from the Yankee. The giant lion remained immobile, lost in a beast dream, still full of the shadows of the cavern.

It was no longer safe to flee. Sydney stood fast, while Kouram and his companion took aim. Three shots sounded. The bullet from the elephant gun creased the lion's skull and burst two hundred feet away. The bullets fired by the two blacks went by harmlessly.

Three enormous leaps; the blond body pounced like a falling rock. It hit the ground where the man had been standing. The sharp blade of the Bowie knife flashed. The elephant gun spoke once more, but in vain, because the forward movement of the beast, as well as his own, had prevented Guthrie from aiming. One of these two lives would soon enter the eternal darkness.

The blacks were taking aim once more, but held their fire. Guthrie was in front of the wild beast, and they weren't sure of their shooting skill.

Guthrie yelled wildly, and the lion answered with a roar. Then they met head-on. The lion stood rock-still, its claws reaching out, its jaws wide open. From them emerged granitelike canines. Guthrie bent down, struck with the great Bowie, plunged its blade to the hilt into the chest and dug in its depths.

And yet the beast did not fall. The claws struck the ribs of the Yankee. The enormous mouth tried to grab the skull of the man. Sydney realized that the Bowie had not reached the heart. He struck the lion's nose with his left fist, and the beast, snarling, drew back. Then, drawing out his weapon, the man hit once more at the shoulder joint.

With harsh breath, the giant man and the giant carnivore fought on stubbornly. Finally, it was the beast that fell. . . .

A shadow floated over Guthrie's eyes. His head had struck a rock, and he was nearly unconscious. And the lioness was merely three bounds away, followed by a black-maned lion. Sydney readied himself for a fight to the death. Before his muscles could come into play, the two beasts would have torn him apart. . . .

However, not far away, Sir George had just come into sight, Phillippe was just coming up over the hill. . . .

Both men aimed and fired at the lioness. The shots had scarcely rung out when the beast turned and fell, hit twice in the head. As she fell, she struck the black-maned lion, and he stopped and smelled the dying lioness. More shots exploded and the black lion, in turn, ceased to know the forest, the savanna, and the intoxicating nights.

The entire caravan had appeared. The blacks were screaming with joy, and Guthrie was standing up. There was no longer any danger. Far away, the giant lion had disappeared beyond the rocks. Fearful, the other beasts had retreated.

"I was not far from knowing what goes on on the other side," Guthrie growled. He was a little pale, bleeding along the ribs, yet full of a joy that he could not hide. He shook the hands of Sir George and Phillippe. "There must not be many riflemen of your class, even in Capetown."

"No," Hareton said, who had just run up with Muriel. "But we definitely must not split up in the future."

"The master is right," Kouram added, "and we must not forget the Stunted Men. Kouram has found traces of them. Kouram would not be surprised if they laid a trap for us!"

8.

The Secret Pursuit

What would have killed a man had only slowed down life in the male great ape. Death had tried hard to get him for its own, but it had failed. The gashes were healing, and the threads that had bound up the torn flesh were about ready to be removed. If the ape suffered any distress from the cavalier manner in which Ironcastle had stuffed its intestines back into its body, it did not show it.

Beneath the bulging bone of brow, from the sunken eyes, interest and alertness once more shone. He often paced back and forth the length of the chain attached to the steel band around his ankle. At times his forehead became wrinkled; images floated in his head, vanished campsites and the shapes of his females. When the men came near, his hair rose, and he threw up his arms to ward off the danger of the unfamiliar.

And yet, there was one that he always welcomed. Whenever Hareton appeared, the forest dweller raised his heavy head and his eyes shone brightly. With increasing fondness, he gazed upon the pale face, the light hair, the hands which had soothed his suffering and which had fed him. In spite of recurring worries and eddies of suspicion, familiarity and beneficial repetition, the origin of all security, were making him regard Ironcastle with less and less distrust. And then, the beast suddenly knew there was, in the vastness of the world, someone from whom it could expect food every day: food, the source of life.

Finally, all distrust was gone, replaced by joy at sight of Ironcastle. When the man appeared, the beast became reassured and even tolerated the nearness of others. But the

63

moment Hareton left, he reverted to the totally wild beast.

The Stunted Men could not be tamed. A hostility that could not be overcome shone in the depths of their eyes. Their faces either remained strangely stiff or grimaced with aversion. They accepted both care and food without a sign of gratitude. Their defiance manifested itself by the long preliminaries that preceded all meals. They smelled and felt all the food interminably. Only Muriel did not awaken their hatred. They looked at her tirelessly and, from time to time, something unutterable twisted their thick lips.

One could sense them eternally watchful. Their eyes gathered in all to be seen. Their ears picked up the slightest sound.

After the adventure with the lions, their vigilance became even more intense. Kouram said one morning: "Their tribe is very close. It is talking to them."

"You've heard voices?" Ironcastle said.

"No, master. Not voices. Signs on the grass. On the ground, on the leaves, and on the water."

"How do you know?"

"I know, master, because the grass is cut periodically or woven, because there are furrows on the ground, because the leaves are turned up or torn off in a way not like that of the beasts' passage. Because there are twigs floating on the water, crossed in a particular way . . . I know, master."

"You don't know what all this means?"

"No, master. I do not know their signs. But they can only think of doing us harm, and the prisoners are becoming dangerous. We must kill them or torture them."

"Why torture them?"

"So they will reveal their secrets."

Ironcastle and his companions were horrified.

"But what can they accomplish?" Guthrie said.

"They can help the free ones to lay traps for us."

"We only have to watch them more closely, keep them bound."

"I do not know, master. Even bound, they will manage to help their tribe."

"If we were to torture them, might they talk?"

"Perhaps . . . one of them is less brave than the others. Why not give it a try?" Kouram said guilelessly. "We can always kill them later."

The whites did not answer, knowing fully the incompatibility between their attitude and his.

"We must listen to Kouram," Ironcastle said after their guide had withdrawn. "In his way, he is a very intelligent man."

"Listen to him, no doubt," Guthrie muttered. "But what more can we do than what we are doing now? Realistically, his advice is the only wise counsel. We should torture them and then kill them."

"You wouldn't do that, Sydney!" Muriel said.

"No, I would not. But it would be legitimate to do so. If only for your sake, Muriel. These men are devilish vermin. Willing to perpetrate any crime. You can be sure that they would not hesitate to cook and eat us."

"Useless words. We won't kill them and we can't torture them," Ironcastle said. "Moreover, they could not reveal anything to us since we cannot understand them."

"Perhaps Kouram understands them."

"No. He can only guess, and that is not enough."

"You're right," Phillippe said. "We won't degrade ourselves. However, what should we do with them? They are a danger."

"Your question is an answer," Sir George said. "Do we free them?"

"No! Not yet. Is it possible, if we join the cunning of the blacks to our own, to frustrate their tricks?"

Ironcastle's eyebrows rose as he looked at Phillippe.

"Since the ground, the grass, the leaves and the water speak, can't we modify the signs?"

"I was thinking of that," Ironcastle said. "There is no doubt that we could do it. Moreover, it's an elementary precaution to cover the eyes of captives during a march or, better still, to wrap something around their heads. During the night, they can be kept inside a tent."

"We should also gag them," Guthrie added. "And plug their ears."

"They will be very miserable," Muriel said.

"Not for long. Kouram claims that they never leave the forest. They've never been seen going farther from the forest than a day's march. And this forest is not endless."

"Let's call Kouram," Sir George said.

Kouram silently listened to them. When they were through, he said, "Very well. Kouram will watch. His followers also. But the cunning of the Stunted Men is without end. An escape is always to be feared. Here is something that I just found."

He showed them leaves from date trees tied together with strands of grass. The tips of some of the leaves had been removed while others had holes pierced in them in a symmetrical fashion.

"One of the captives dropped this close to a bush. And it certainly means something evil. Why not kill them?"

The surveillance became more meticulous and more rigid. During the day, the faces of the captives were kept covered. During the night, two sentries stood guard outside their tent. Though they were allowed to walk around in the camp, their legs were shackled. In spite of all this, they were a constant cause of worry.

Despite the Stunted Men's impassiveness, Ironcastle, Phillippe and Muriel began to read certain expressions in which they could recognize their hatred and hopes. At night, low voices rumbled in the tent. In the daytime, sly menace seemed to subtly mask their faces. The least patient of them had spoken words that all guessed to be insulting.

Suddenly, they appeared to have resigned themselves to their fate. In the bivouac area, sitting near the fires, they seemed to dream mysteriously, as still as corpses.

"Well," Phillippe asked Kouram one night, "are they still talking to their fellow tribesmen?"

"They still are," Kouram replied gravely. "They listen and they answer."

"But how?"

"They hear through the voice of the jackal, of the crows, of the hyenas, of the leopards. Perhaps of the trees. And they answer through the ground."

"But aren't you removing their signs?"

"We are, master. But not all of them, because we don't know them all. The Stunted Men are more cunning than we are."

This night was rendered even more charming by the soft wind which came in from the land toward the lake. The flames of the fires were sending up more firefly-like sparks; soft animal voices whispered in the depths of the forest. Phillippe was studying the Southern Cross, which duplicated itself tremblingly in the waters. Muriel stood next to him. Wrapped in a reddish light mixed with the blue shadows, she seemed like a wavering mirage. He breathed in her fragrance. She awoke in him all that is mysterious in the hearts of men.

"Nothing," he said, "reminds me less of a night in Touraine. Yet, this night does make me think of a night in Touraine . . . a night on the shore of the Loire, close to the castle of Chambord and as reassuring as this one is dreadful."

"Why dreadful?"

"Here, all nights are dreadful. Nature has not lost any of its dark fascination."

"That's true," the young girl whispered. "I believe that we will eventually regret these nights."

"And still," he added with a somewhat anguished tone, "you have managed to enthrall us with your beauty! We could not have encountered more intense sweetness. With you, Muriel, we did completely leave the world where men are masters . . . with you here, our tents become homes . . . our evening fires are like a hearth . . . you are the living image of what humanity has achieved to the utmost, as far as charm and solace are concerned . . . our best hope and our most tender solicitude!"

She was listening to him, curious, strangely moved and knowing that he was in love with her. But, she was troubled deep in her heart, still uncertain about preferring Phillippe to all other men. She thought it better to remain uncommitted.

"You mustn't exaggerate," she said. "I'm not that important. And I'm more often a burden than a consolation."

"I'm not exaggerating, Muriel. Even if you weren't so

radiant and robust, it would be an incomparable boon to see you sitting among us, so far from civilization."

"Well," she murmured, "that's enough talk about *me* for one evening. I wish you would rather look at the stars, shivering gently in the waters of the lake."

And she began to sing softly:

"Twinkle, twinkle, little star,

"How I wonder what you are!"

She added, "I can see myself as a little girl, in front of the lake at home. It was evening, also. A voice was singing that innocent song."

She stopped talking and turned her head, and both of them saw a crawling shape that went rapidly through the firelit zone and threw itself into the lake.

"A prisoner has escaped!" Phillippe shouted.

Kouram, two blacks, and Sir George ran up. They stood gazing out at the surface of the waters. Dark forms were moving about; reptiles, batrachians, and fish. But no human shape could be seen.

"The canoes," Hareton said.

The collapsible boats were assembled in a few minutes. Two crews, wearing the armor-garments, criss-crossed the lake, but the search was in vain.

The Stunted Man had made good his escape or else he had drowned. They were unable to find out how he had managed it.

"You see, master?" Kouram said after the canoes had come back to the shore.

"I see," Ironcastle said slowly, "that you were quite right. That Stunted Man was more cunning than we were."

"Not him alone, master. His tribe freed him."

"His tribe?" Guthrie said incredulously.

"His tribe, master. It gave him the weapon to cut his bonds. And perhaps the water that burns."

"What *is* this burning water?"

"It is a water that comes out of the ground, master. It burns grass, wood, wool and flesh. If the Stunted Men have poured some into the hollow of a rock, the fugitive might have used it."

"We shall see."

The ground beneath the tent showed no sign of any corrosive substance.

"Kouram loves fairy tales," Guthrie growled.

"No," Sir George said. "Here are fragments of rope that have evidently been burned."

He held up a strand. Its tip had been burned.

Ironcastle's eyebrows rose.

"This is extremely important. Kouram was not exaggerating."

"What proof do we have that the rope was burned with a corrosive?" Sydney asked. "The captive might have managed to use an overlooked brand from the fire."

"No," Sir George said. He was still examining the fragment of rope. "This was not burned by fire."

"Then why have they held off so long using their damned liquid?"

"Because the water that burns cannot be found everywhere, master," Kouram said. "You can walk for weeks and even months without finding it."

"We made a mistake by not bringing dogs," Phillippe said.

"Before we left, we should have had some brought over from the Antilles, but we didn't have time," Hareton said.

"We can always train jackals," Guthrie said, half-serious and half-joking.

"I'd rather trust the ape," Ironcastle retorted. "He has a deep hatred for these Stunted Men."

"You are right, master," Kouram said. "The man-who-does-not-talk is the enemy of the Stunted Men."

"Do you think that we can train him?"

"You can, master, and you alone."

Hareton got to work training the anthropoid. At first, nothing seemed to penetrate the thick skull. When he was brought close to the captives, the beast became extraordinarily agitated and his fluorescent eyes became rounder. Turning green, they expressed both a threatening fury and a mysterious fear.

But, after a few days, a sort of mental explosion occurred, just like the sudden blooming of certain tropical flowers. He learned by leaps and bounds. He seemed to positively understand that he was supposed to watch the prisoners. Hareton unshackled him.

The ape thereafter stayed close to their tent, smelling their terrible odors and keeping a close watch on the surroundings.

One evening, while Hareton was contemplating the fire, Kouram appeared in front of him. "Master, the man-with-out-words has felt the coming of the Stunted Men. They are close to the camp."

"Is everyone at his post?"

"Yes, master. But it is not an attack that we should fear."

"What then?"

"I do not know. We must watch the food, the captives, and the ground."

"The ground? Why?"

"The Stunted Men know about hidden caves. Their ancestors dug them long ago."

Hareton understood what the black meant. Thoughtful, he went over to the ape. He found him to be violently agitated, listening and sniffing everywhere. The hair covering the nape of his neck rose intermittently.

"Well, Sylvius?"

Hareton gently rubbed the shoulder of the beast. Sylvius answered with a hesitant gesture, almost a caress, and a low cry came from his throat.

"Go, Sylvius!"

The beast headed for the western end of the camp. He became frantic and, bending down, began to dig in the ground.

"You see, master," Kouram said, who had come up to them. "The Stunted Men are in the earth."

"Then the camp is right over a cavern?"

"Yes, master."

Hareton stood for a length of time, deeply worried. Kouram was lying prone and had his ear close to the ground.

"They are right there."

The growls of Sylvius confirmed his words.

A scream of fear tore through the night, the scream of a woman.

"It's Muriel!" he shouted.

He began to run toward her tent. The black who had been guarding Muriel was lying on the ground, unmoving. Hareton raised the canvas curtain which protected the entrance to the tent and the beam of his flashlight shone inside.

Muriel was not in it.

9.

Muriel in the Night

In the center of the tent was an oval hole large enough for two men to pass through at once. Next to it could be seen a block of green porphyry.

Hareton, shouting with alarm, darted forward. Almost formless steps went down into the darkness. Without hesitation, Hareton stepped down. Upon reaching the last step, he saw before him an underground passage, but a dozen paces away it ended in a cave-in of dirt and rocks.

By this time, Phillippe, Sydney and Sir George had come down also.

"Damn it!" Guthrie yelled, "I'll kill them all!"

"We must get organized," Sir George said.

Phillippe's head was swimming; his heart was beating like an alarm bell. All were feeling around the surrounding earth in the hope of finding an exit.

"Kouram," Sir George said, "bring shovels and picks."

Guthrie, after a moment's fury, quit raving.

"My drill!" he said.

He had foreseen, before they left, the possibility of an obstacle, either of rocks or earth, that would need such a tool. Accompanied by Dick and Patrick, he went to get it. It was an ingenious machine, which could be worked either with gasoline or by hand. Relatively light, only two men were needed to carry it around. Sydney filled its tank and carried the machine down into the hole. He started it, and it roared as it dug a passage thirty times as fast as could have been done with shovels and picks. In three minutes, its point broke through a shield of three-inch-thick stone placed by the Stunted Men.

Hareton was the first to go through the hole. The beams of their flashlights showed no trace of the recent presence of Muriel and the Stunted Men. They soon had to bend down. Then the fissure became so narrow that it was impossible to move forward two abreast.

"It's up to me to go first," Guthrie said in an imperious tone. "No, Uncle, no!" he added, grabbing Hareton. "Here, my strength is our best advantage. I will smash through any obstacle more easily than any of you, and I will be better able to beat anyone who might dare to attack us."

"But," Hareton said, "the passage might become too narrow for you."

"Then I will lie down, and you will pass over my body."

Guthrie was arguing as he walked forward. It was logical for him to go ahead of the others. Along with Sir George and Patrick, he had donned the spear-proof clothing.

Although it became lower still, the passage did not narrow any further. The pursuers were bending down so low that they were almost crawling. Then the ceiling began to rise and the passage widened. Sir George cried out. He had just picked up Muriel's small handkerchief.

Hareton grabbed it and pressed it to his lips.

"At least we are now certain that she passed through here," Guthrie said.

A faint ray of light penetrated into the underground corridor. Suddenly, the lake showed itself beneath a crescent of moon.

For several minutes, the group of men contemplated the waters in which were gently reflected Orion, Sirius, Virgo, and the Southern Cross. Jackals were howling on the plain; giant frogs raised voices as mighty as those of buffaloes.

"Nothing," Sir George murmured.

Three islands spread their tree-covered masses before them.

"That's where they must have taken her," Hareton said plaintively. Tears were running down his cheeks. His usually impassive face was dissolving in his anguish.

"I did an unforgivable thing . . . I should be horse-whipped."

Phillippe's despair was equal to his. A nameless horror settled down upon him, and his feeling of uselessness made it even more intolerable.

Guthrie shook both fists toward the island.

"We can do nothing here," Sir George said. "We will lose any chance that we have of finding her if we stay here where they can see us."

He looked along the clifflike shore of the islands. Climbing up them would be suicidal. It was almost certain that the Stunted Men were hidden up there. They would slaughter all those not protected by the armored clothing. Here, under an overhanging cliff, and with the lake empty as far as the islands, surprise was impossible.

"What can we do?" Hareton asked.

In the grip of anguish and sorrow, he felt a deep need for giving the command to someone with a cooler mind.

"There is only one thing to do. Go back to camp the same way we came. Then we will man the rafts and explore these islands."

"Right," Guthrie said. His first excitement was making way for the instincts of the huntsman. "Let's leave to chance only what we have no control over. Let's do it fast. I'm leaving last, after all of you."

"No," Sir George objected. "For the retreat, Sydney, it would be best if I covered you. I can turn about more rapidly if I have to face the enemy."

Sydney yielded. The small troop went back the way it had come, moving rapidly underground. When they reached the drill, the Englishman murmured, "We are in luck. The exit could have been blocked."

It took over half an hour to ready the collapsible canoe. Inwardly, Hareton and Phillippe were in a state of anguish because of Muriel. But outwardly, they acted with a furious but cool energy. Like Guthrie, they knew that they must not lose a second in the pursuit.

Sir George was to keep watch over the camp, aided by Patrick, Dick, and most of the Africans. The expedition was comprised of Ironcastle, Guthrie, Phillippe, four blacks including Kouram, and the anthropoid. The latter would be used to track down the Stunted Men through his keen sense of smell and hearing.

The blacks had donned garments made of heavy tarpaulin. This should stop any spears cast at them, but the ape had refused any sort of protection.

Before they left, they made a necessary experiment. Sylvius was allowed to roam freely, and he headed directly for the underground passage. His behavior indicated that it was unlikely that the Stunted Men would appear on the surface, at least close to the camp. The abduction of Muriel by way of the cliff seemed unlikely. Everything pointed toward an escape via the lake.

"Let's get on board," Guthrie said, "since we have to make a choice."

The motor coughed, sputtered, then caught hold, and the small craft made its way rapidly over the quiet waters. It stopped at the first island, where Ironcastle, Guthrie and Phillippe disembarked with the anthropoid. He was showing signs of irritation.

"They came through here," Hareton said. A saurian jumped into the lake, furtive beasts slithered through the fog, and a bird with long wings flew through the boughs.

The man of the woods, having smelled the ground, loped across the island.

"He's free," Guthrie growled. "He only has to climb up in the trees and we'll never see him again."

The ape crossed the island diagonally and stopped before a small creek. Phillippe picked up a shining object among the reeds. It was a pin made from a shell.

"Muriel," Hareton said, and he groaned.

The anthropoid growled but did not move. Hareton put a hand on his shoulder, and the ape made a gesture that was almost human.

"There's no doubt," Guthrie said. "Those rats have gone farther. Let's visit the other islands."

There were three main islands and several islets. The explorers found no trace of the Stunted Men.

"Lord," Hareton prayed. His hands were joined together and held up toward the stars. "Have pity on Muriel . . . take my life and spare hers!"

10.

The Men of the Stars

Wammha, the Blue-Eagle, climbed up the baobab. Three huts in the branches held his wives, his daughters, and his sons. The Blue-Eagle had snowy places in the dark wool of his hair, but there was still strength in his arms, courage in his breast, and cunning in his granite-hard skull.

His amber eyes gazed over the palm trees, the pandanus, the fig trees, and the rest of the surrounding forest. The baobabs formed large islands among the rest. From century to century, they bore the huts of the Goura-Zannkas, Men-of-the-Stars. Cone-shaped, resembling termite nests, these huts were strong protection against the sun and the rain. Wammha was in command of the five clans of this tribe. It comprised five hundred warriors, armed with stone axes, clubs, and spears. There were other tribes farther away, toward the east, and still others in the valley of the dead. They were always at war because of the need for more and more hunting territory. The captives were eaten. At times, the tribes became allies in order to beat the Stunted Men, who looked with envy upon their lands.

But this year the war had just ended. Wammha's men had beaten the sons of the Red Rhinoceros and of the Black Lion and had captured fifty warriors and sixty women. The feast was being prepared and would continue until the new moon. The captives had been immersed to the neck in the lake. They would stay there until it was time to slit their throats. Thus, their flesh would be tenderer and tastier.

The fires rose in the Great Clearing. Wammha knew the necessary words to appease the Mighty Things which dwell

76

in the Water, in the Earth, in the Wind, and in the Sun. He accompanied them with the required gestures.

The Goura-Zannkas knew the Hierarchy of Forces. There are those which, in the Invisible World, resemble men or beasts; they are the smallest and least to be feared. Then there are those that look like the great trees; their power is unfathomable. Those that have no form and no limit, that change and draw away, that grow small and become huge, use as their language the storm, the thunder, the fire, and the flood. They are not beings but rather Things; facing them, beings can do nothing!

When Wammha was up in the baobab, he yelled violently. His sons showed themselves, along with his sons-in-law, assembled in the center of the branches.

Then Wammha spoke:

"Sons of the chosen clans . . . the first clans of the air . . . whose master is Wammha, hark to my command! One warrior out of ten will travel west, north, east, and on the lake. Unknown men are coming. Many are strange-looking and resemble neither the sons of the Stars, the sons of the Red Rhinoceros or the Black Lion, nor of the Swamp. They do not even look like the Stunted Men. Their faces have no color, their hair shines like straw, and their weapons are incomprehensible. Our warriors will surround their caravan. Tonight, they will be camping close to our border . . . we will wipe them out, or we will become their allies! . . . Ba-Luama will lead the warriors. And tomorrow, Wammha will follow him with three hundred men. I have spoken!"

Ba-Luama thus gathered one warrior out of ten, first under the baobab of the Blue-Eagle, then from all over the forest. They left to surround the men with colorless faces.

"It is well," said the Blue-Eagle once the expedition was on its way. "Let victory be consecrated."

Hegum, the Man-with-the-Horn-that-Made-Noise, blew toward the four corners of the Heavens; the clans gathered in the Great Clearing, where the mighty voice of Blue-Eagle resounded.

"The Goura-Zannkas are masters of the forest and of the lake. The sons of the Black Lion and of the Red Rhinoceros have stood up against us. We have broken their skulls, opened their bellies, and pierced their hearts. Their entrails fell upon the ground, and their blood ran like a red river. We have captured many warriors, women, and children. Twenty warriors who have soaked in the lake all night and all day are ready for the Great Sacrifice!"

A mighty cry went up from the clans. Yet they were not truly bloodthirsty. When the war spear was at rest, they did not chafe, they were content, and they did not attack other tribes. But, war being sacred, it was their duty to eat captives.

"Let the fires be lit," Blue-Eagle said.

It was done, and their light fought against the fugitive glimmer of the dusk and was stronger than the light of the rising moon, half of which was silver and half ashes.

Brandishing torches, the clans went down to the lake. Only the heads of the captives could be seen; their feet were tied to blocks of granite. Seeing the torches, they knew what was to come. But they did not cry out, and their faces were expressionless.

"Sons of the Red Rhinoceros and sons of the Black Lion!" shouted Wammha. "On the day of his birth, man is already close to the day of his death. Where are all those ancestors without numbers? And soon where will be those of us who lead you to the sacrifice? Your death is fine and glorious, sons of the Rhinoceros and sons of the Lion. You have fought for your clans, and we have fought for ours. Many sons of the Eagle have fallen under your spears. We have no hatred for you, but we must obey all Things, because Things are everything and beings are nothing."

The captives were pulled from the mud. Since their legs were paralyzed by the tight bonds and the cold water, they had to be carried to the fires. They laughed when the women, according to the millennia-old custom, brought them millet cakes. The meal of the vanquished is as sacred as the meal of the victors. The sons of the Black Lion and of the Red Rhinoceros forgot their impending death and ate the cakes.

Wammha gave the signal for the ritual dances. A warrior, his face painted as red as if dipped in blood, beat on a wooden drum, while two men blew into reed flutes. The blows fell in an odd rhythm, sounding hollow, accompanied by the monotonous chant of the flutes. Some warriors began to twist their bodies to and fro. The music of the flutes accelerated, the hollow sounds came faster and faster, the eyes of the dancers were lit with a feverish gleam, while the bodies were swinging with the rhythm of the music. Then the women joined the men.

The drums sounded frenetically, the flutes yelped like jackals, and the Goura-Zannkas mixed together in a wild saraband. They linked arms, shouted piercing cries, formed a moving mass or rolled on the ground, bellowing, screaming and howling. They were biting one another, and blood was flowing on their dark chests.

Standing on a mound, immobile, with an impassive face, Wammha gazed upon the spectacle. When the fury threatened to become homicidal, he shouted thrice, formidably. Suddenly, there was a profound silence. The pearly moon seemed to be lowering itself onto the tip of the baobabs; the light from the fires eclipsed the stars; the captives, having been fed, awaited death.

The Blue-Eagle gave the signal. Armed with the green sacrificial knives, some warriors came forward. Many captives, losing their stoicism, wailed hollowly and tried to rise or stretched out their hands in supplication.

Every warrior had reached his intended victim and then fixed his gaze upon Wammha. When the chief's hand rose, the knives slit the throats, and a redness gushed over the ferns. The eyes of the vanquished ceased to roll in their sockets, the bodies lay limply. The thighs, the arms, the heads, the trunks roasted in the night, and the Goura-Zannkas knew the delicious joy of devouring the enemy.

After it was all over, the Blue-Eagle gave an order. At the time when the stars would extinguish themselves in the four corners of the heavens, the Goura-Zannkas would rise in strength to give battle to the phantom-warriors.

11.

The Warlike Dawn

Two-thirds of the night had gone by. Kouram kept watch over the fires, rising now and then to walk around and smell the wide-open spaces. He knew that the Stunted Men were no longer close to the camp since they had taken Muriel away. But he could guess at other dangers, for Humra, the keenest of the black scouts, thought that he had seen men in the bush.

Kouram, having sent Humra and two others to reconnoiter, asked himself if he should wake the chief. None of the whites, except for Patrick, was up, and Kouram did not think it necessary to warn him. Although he judged him to be powerful in combat, he thought him not very intelligent.

Situated on the lakeshore in a cut surrounded by fires, the camp was ready for battle. At the first sound of danger, the whites as well as the blacks would be at their posts. Kouram had an almost religious trust in the wisdom of his chief, in the repeating rifles, in the elephant gun, and most of all in the frightening machine gun. But they must not let themselves be surprised. The shore of the lake did not allow for a direct attack and, beyond the fires, there was a grassy surface where no man could hide. The nearest cover was five hundred paces away. No matter what the enemy's tactics might be, they could not come close without showing themselves.

The stars went on their way, and the Southern Cross straightened out in the direction of the pole. Then the shadowy figures of the scouts appeared, and Humra showed himself in the firelight. He had the light body of a jackal and the yellow eyes of a vulture.

He said, "Humra has seen men on the side where the sun goes down and where the Seven Stars shine."

"Are they many in numbers?"

"They are greater in numbers than we. Humra could not count them. Humra does not think they will attack before the stars flee the coming light."

"Why does Humra think this?"

"Because most of them are asleep. If they did not wait for other warriors, they would try to surprise us during the night."

Kouram lowered his head in deep thought. Those were true words. He looked at the east. The stars, clear upon a very dark sky, were the same as before a single man or beast had come into being on the face of the earth. However, Kouram knew that within an hour the day would extinguish them one by one.

The silence was at once mighty and soft. The beasts which had to die in order for their flesh to renew the flesh of others had died. Even the voices of the jackals were quiet.

Kouram, having received the reports of the other scouts, checked the fires and passed close to the sentries.

Patrick, who was on duty at the southern point of the camp, said, "What did they find out?"

"Some men are watching us."

"The Stunted Men?"

"No, others who have come from the forest."

Patrick looked surprised. This savage was actually looking forward to combat.

"You expect them to attack us?"

"They will attack if they feel strong enough."

"Too bad for them," the Irishman growled.

"We will kill them all," Kouram said. He strode to the chief's tent, raised the curtain, and called in.

Hareton had been sleeping lightly since the disappearance of Muriel. He got up, put on some clothes, then spoke.

"What do you want, Kouram?"

There was faint hope in that question; any event, any word, any thought brought Muriel to his mind. Grief tore through him. In the space of a few days, his flesh seemed to have melted away. Remorse mixed with his sorrow. Because he had taken Muriel with him, he felt as guilty as if he had killed her.

"Master," Kouram said, "the camp is surrounded."

"By the Stunted Men?" Hareton shouted. His apathy had suddenly become a boiling anger.

"No, master, by black men. Humra thinks they came from the forest."

"Are they in great numbers?"

"Humra did not manage to count them. They are hiding."

Hareton lowered his head and then said, "I would like to make an alliance with them!"

"That would be good," Kouram said. "But how can we talk to them?"

He did not mean that it was impossible to understand them or to be understood by them. He was versed in the universal sign language, having practiced it from childhood.

"They will throw their spears at anyone trying to approach them," he said. "However, master, I will try it as soon as the day comes."

The stars were shining feebly. The dawn was near. The sun would appear soon.

"I don't want you to risk your life."

A slightly ironical smile wrinkled Kouram's purple lips.

"Kouram will not risk his life." He added naively, "Kouram does not want to die."

Hareton walked around the camp and then checked the machine gun.

"I should have brought more than one," he thought.

He took a good look at the site, the lake where the stars were spreading their twinkling lights, the plain, the brush, the distant forest. It was a peaceful hour. Nature, sullen yet holding promises of happiness, made Hareton's heart beat horribly fast even as he breathed the velvet air.

He turned toward the Southern Cross and prayed, "O Lord, God of my salvation, I have cried day and night before Thee. . . ."

He kept on praying, mixing despair with hope and faith.

His hollow eyes shone feverishly. Remorse continued to bite his heart deeply.

The tropical dawn appeared and vanished in an instant. Daybreak rapidly spread the light. The sun, copper-hued, rose above the waters of the lake.

"Should we call them now?" Kouram said.

"Yes."

Kouram went to get a strange flute, cut from a young papyrus reed, resembling those used by some inhabitants of the Great Forest. From it came a soft sound that carried far and wide.

Then, signaling to Humra, who was following him, he left the camp. They traveled for two hundred paces over the plain and then stopped. Nobody could have come within a spear-cast without their seeing them. Kouram took his flute and drew from it some monotonous sounds, full of melancholy. Then his voice rose resoundingly, "The men from the camp want to make friends with their hidden brothers! Let them come forth and show themselves."

He did not hope to be understood by men who spoke an unknown language. But, like countless generations of savage and civilized men, he believed in the value of the spoken word and its evocative powers.

Neither brush nor savanna showed signs of human presence. Some antelope moved slowly in the distance, and the diurnal birds celebrated in their own manner the life-giving light.

"Why don't you answer?" Kouram shouted. "We know that your warriors are besieging our camp. Humra of the eagle eyes has seen you on the side of the Seven Stars and on the side where the sun sets."

Still no answer—but a sound came from deep in the brush. Humra, whose hearing was as sharp as his eyesight, said, "I think, chief full of wisdom, that other warriors are coming."

Kouram, simultaneously in the grip of worry and anger, said menacingly, "Let not the hidden men put too much faith in their numbers! The white chiefs have weapons as terrible as an earthquake or as the fire that devours the forest!"

He accompanied his words with gestures but he went on in softer tones, "We do not come as enemies. If you wish to become our allies, your chiefs will be welcome in our camp."

Suddenly, a black man rose, bellowing like a buffalo. He held a spear in one hand and a club in the other. His chest was deep as a gorilla's, his jaw jutted like the boss of a shield, his yellow eyes shone with fanaticism.

He cried out several words in an unknown tongue, but his gestures were easily interpreted. There was nothing of friendliness in them.

"The men of the camp are invincible," Kouram answered through sign language.

Wammha, the Blue-Eagle, laughed in a haughty and mocking manner. He shouted twice, and the Goura-Zannka warriors stood up among the bushes, the ferns, and the tall grass. They were mighty men, young and tall. Quickly, silently, they surrounded the entire camp. Hegum, the Man-with-the-Horn, blew toward the rising sun. The Sons of the Stars gave a great roar and shook their clubs and spears.

Wammha said, with gestures and with words, "The Sons-of-the-Stars have ten warriors for each of yours! We will take the camp, along with your animals and your treasures. And we will eat the men!"

Kouram, understanding that the black chief wanted war, spread his arms, held them out before him, then pointed to the ground. Lowering himself, he said, "The men of the forest will die like the insects that rise during the evening over the waters of the lake."

The resounding voice of the Blue-Eagle alternated with the horn of Hegum.

The Goura-Zannkas began to form four columns, each comprising about fifty men.

Kouram made a final attempt. His voice and his gestures spoke together, "It is still possible to become allies."

But the Blue-Eagle, seeing his columns in battle order, felt the power of war surge through him. He gave the signal for the assault.

The camp was ready to fight them. On the mound, Iron-castle and a black were manning the machine gun. Sydney was checking the elephant gun. Phillippe and Sir George were watching the south and the east. The others, ready to open fire, formed an elliptical line.

"Don't kill their chief!" Ironcastle shouted. He still hoped to make an alliance with Wammha, even after a battle.

The horn of the Goura-Zannkas sounded over the lake. Kouram ran back to the camp as two hundred wild men charged.

"Fire!" Ironcastle yelled.

The machine gun, swiveling, discharged a stream of bullets so close together that they seemed like a liquid spurt. The elephant gun boomed. Sir George and Phillippe were aiming methodically, aided by the fire of the skirmishers.

It was a slaughter. Before the Goura-Zannkas had managed to cross half the distance separating them from the camp, more than sixty warriors were lying on the ground. The machine gun was knocking them down in lines; the elephant gun was scattering them in sheaves of blood, flesh, bones, and entrails. Each shot fired by Phillippe or Sir George knocked down a man.

The .577 express rifle accomplished the first rout. The black column which attacked along the lake, finding their warriors torn to bits, heads and limbs thrown about, panicked and fled among the papyrus reeds. Then the machine gun stopped the group that was coming from the south, while Phillippe and Sir George, aided by Dick and the blacks, riddled the third column.

But in the west, the force led by Blue-Eagle was still formidable. The chief ran ahead, brandishing his axe and his spear, he and the mass close behind him only two hundred yards away.

Hareton watched them come. These were the elite, young warriors full of battle-passion, tall, and well-muscled. If they managed to break into the camp, they would massacre everybody.

Ironcastle had about sixty seconds to break up the charge.

"Too bad," he growled.

With regret, he turned the machine gun around toward

the west. Methodically, he sprayed bullets at the enemy. It was as if blades of fire or streaks of lightning had raked the attackers. Men were running around like bees in the smoke, falling down with screams of anger or pain, or fleeing haphazardly. Soon, Wammha had only ten warriors behind him. Hareton got rid of them with a single sweep of the gun.

The Blue-Eagle stood alone facing the camp. Death flapped its wings around him, covered him with its shadow. All the immense strength of his race, in a single moment, had become like the weakness of the jackal facing a lion. All that had made his chest rise with pride, all the glory had vanished before a mysterious power. His pride sank into a humility without depth.

He raised his spear and his club, then shouted, "Kill Wammha! But let a warrior's hand pierce his chest! Who will fight Wammha?"

His words were brave, but his voice sounded sad and mournful. Kouram, standing close to Guthrie, understood his gestures.

"He wants combat."

Guthrie, laughing, looked around. He could only see some fugitives and many dead and wounded.

"I will give him that consolation."

The giant man leaped over a mound of hot ashes and, armed with an axe, charged forward to meet the Blue-Eagle. The Goura-Zannka chief, astonished, watched him come. Even though the clans of the Stars had many men of tall stature, none of them were as tall as this pale man, whose strength must be that of the rhinoceros. A superstitious sadness weighted down the soul of the chief while Guthrie shouted, "You want to fight? Here I am!"

Wammha hurled his spear, and it brushed against Sydney's shoulder without even damaging the protective cloth. A few leaps; the Yankee was before the black. The Blue-Eagle yelled fiercely and raised his club. Guthrie laughed.

The club fell, but Sydney's axe bit deeply into the wood and tore the weapon from the hands of the chief.

"You have done battle," he said, and laughed. "Now come."

Grabbing Wammha, he threw him over his shoulder and carried him away like a child. The people in the camp cheered. The fleeing Goura-Zannkas stopped, gripped by fear and awe. Those who had hidden in the reeds or bushes wailed, overcome by the marvel they had just witnessed.

"Here you are," Guthrie said, lowering his paralyzed burden to the ground.

Wammha was trembling. A thousand times he had risked his life. No man could have better resisted torture and impassively awaited the hour when he would be eaten by the enemy. The fear that kept him spellbound was not that of the warrior who fears death, but that of a man facing the inconceivable. On Guthrie's shoulder, he had felt as weak as a little child. And out there, nearly a hundred Goura-Zannkas lay dead or wounded, while none in the camp had even been scratched. It was as if all the spears and the clubs since the Beginning, weapons which had killed men without numbers, as well as buffaloes and boars, and which had sometimes even felled lions, had suddenly been transformed into blades of straw.

Silent, ashen, Wammha remained prone. A voice drew him up from his dejection.

Slowly, he raised his head. Kouram was talking and gesturing at him. And because Kouram was also black, he felt less crushed.

Kouram, with speech and sign language, was saying, "Do the men of the forest now want to become the friends of the men who come from the north and the east?"

He repeated his words and his signs until Wammha understood them. Wammha was astounded and bewildered. He could not conceive that, being a captive, he was not destined to be a warriors' feast.

He looked at Kouram, Ironcastle, and especially at the colossal adversary who had carried him away like a child. Because he had imagination, he managed to overcome the limits of his beliefs. Men so different from the Goura-Zannkas, and so strangely and awfully armed, could have strange customs. Furthermore, cunning suggested that, being mere passers-through, the strangers had little interest in leaving enemies behind them. Curiosity also, a curiosity

sharp, passionate, and impetuous, animated Blue-Eagle.
What could he lose? Was not his life already in the hands
of his conquerors? And Wammha estimated his life to be
worth that of a hundred warriors.

Abruptly, his hesitation faded. He turned toward the
giant and made a gesture of consent. The alliance was now
a fact.

12.

Stunted Men and Goura-Zannkas

Though their new allies seemed to accept thoroughly their defeat, the vigilance of the conquerors did not as yet relax. They camped near the trees of the Men-of-the-Stars in an open place near a river, but at all times at least a fourth of them stood guard.

The defeated gathered to look upon the strangers but kept their distance. Men, women, and children avidly watched the fantastic beings who had won a battle without one being struck by club or spear. The strangers were not hated because of their victory. A religious respect was mixed with the fear they inspired. Guthrie especially awed the Goura-Zannkas. They said among themselves, "He is the strongest of all men. He has the might of Things."

This admiration spread to Hareton, who, after a few days, walked among them unguarded. And, the most linguistically capable of the group, he quickly learned the Goura-Zannka tongue. Mainly, he talked to the Blue-Eagle.

He learned that the Men-of-the-Stars and the Stunted Men had been implacable enemies since the beginning of time. Tradition and legend told tales of combat, defeats and victories, the cunning of the Stunted Men against the cunning of the clans. But, for almost an entire generation, the red, the black, and the blue Stunted Men had not been seen. When Wammha realized that one of their tribes was near, he shook with fury, and his eyes shone like those of the leopard in the dusk.

Hareton understood the chief's reaction. Their alliance was based on something primitive and indestructible, something that went beyond war among men.

"The Blue-Eagle will find the captive," the chief said many times. "He will seek her over the waters, in the ground, and among the rocks. The Goura-Zannkas are more cunning than jackals."

The American decided to show him their two captives. When he saw them, he leaped forward and raised his club to smash their skulls, but Kouram stopped him.

"Can you talk to them?" Ironcastle said to Blue-Eagle.

The hate which animated the Blue-Eagle was mirrored on the dull faces of the prisoners. Wammha kept insulting them tirelessly. Through the centuries of combat, the two races had learned to understand each other, at least on a basic level.

"Can you talk to them?" Ironcastle repeated.

"The Blue-Eagle knows how to talk to them."

Hareton said, in a voice that shook with hope, "Ask them what their people have done with the young girl that they took away."

Ironcastle and Kouram repeated the question many times, the former with words, the latter by gestures.

Wammha called out to the captives. Sly and silent laughter twisted their monstrous mouths. One of the captives spoke, "The Phantom-Men will never again see the girl with the hair of light. She is now living with the Stunted Men in the earth and on the earth. She is the slave of a chief."

"Where are the Stunted Men?" the Blue-Eagle yelled.

"They are everywhere," the other said, describing a circle with his hand.

Wammha threatened them with his club, but the Stunted Men remained impassive.

Once the Blue-Eagle had translated the answer, a tragic silence fell on the assembly. The vision of Muriel as a prisoner among those brutes made her despairing father cry out in distress.

"The captives will tell me where the horde is," the Goura-Zannka chieftain said.

"Never!"

"We must burn their feet," Kouram said. "Then, they will speak."

The Blue-Eagle nodded, but he also said that no torture could make the Stunted Men talk.

"Then, we must kill them," Kouram said. "If it were not for them, the daughter of the chief would not have been taken away. And without them, perhaps the Stunted Men would have given up pursuit."

It was logical, but they had to forget what might have been.

"Would you like to help us find the Stunted Men?" Hareton asked.

The black chief breathed in deeply and he shouted, "Wammha wants to exterminate them!" He brandished his club above the heads of the captives.

The captives closed their eyes as if they expected to be brained at once.

Like Kouram, the Blue-Eagle yelled, "We must kill them!"

"If we let them live," the chief said, "even with their eyes covered, their lips sealed, and their limbs tied with ropes, even wrapped in a bag, they will talk to the others."

"We cannot kill unarmed men," Hareton said. "No matter how much they deserve to die."

Kouram and Wammha looked at each other, an unspoken complicity in their eyes.

"What will Wammha do to find the Stunted Men?" Hareton said.

"The warriors will search the forest, the earth, and the waters. The sorcerers will consult the Clouds, the Winds and the Stars. And the Goura-Zannkas know all the caves."

"If the Blue-Eagle succeeds, he will get the weapon that kills three thousand paces away," Ironcastle said, pointing to a rifle.

The yellow eyes shone like the star Aldebaran.

Ten minutes later, the Man-with-the-Horn sounded the gathering of the warriors.

Before the evening, the Goura-Zannkas knew that the Stunted Men were close to the camp. But they were underground, since the earth was full of natural caves, often joined together by the works of the ancestors of the Stunted

Men, before the Sons-of-the-Stars had conquered the three forests and the western side of the lake.

Wammha said, "This night, the Goura-Zannkas will fight! They will win. But they will be surer of victory if the Phantom-Men bring their thunder weapons."

A loud clamor interrupted him; a group of Goura-Zannkas was dragging in two prisoners. Even in the shadows, the chests and buffalolike faces could be recognized.

The Blue-Eagle smiled ferociously.

"Now, the battle is near! These will give us their hearts."

Hareton shivered. "They are prisoners!"

"Prisoners must be eaten! It is the will of the Earth, the Waters, and the Ancestors."

Ironcastle translated for the others the black chief's speech.

"It's their business. You have to respect the laws of your allies," Guthrie said.

Sir George and Phillippe remained silent.

Coldly, Wammha gave an order. Clubs rose, and the Stunted Men fell, their skulls shattered.

"It would have been better to let them soak in the sacred waters first," Wammha said, regretfully.

Seeing that Hareton did not understand him, he added, "I had them killed so that *you* would not feel any regret."

"That savage is full of delicate sensibilities," Sydney said after Ironcastle had translated for them.

Wammha laughed. Looking at Guthrie, he said, "To vanquish the Stunted Men, will the Phantom-Leaders assist us with their Thunder Weapons?"

Ironcastle translated this for his comrades.

"We have to run that risk," Sir George said.

"What risk? The risk of doing battle?" Guthrie said. "We cannot avoid it."

"The risk of treachery," Hareton said. "But I don't believe they would betray us."

"I'm sure they wouldn't," Phillippe said.

"No," Kouram added, gravely. "They will be faithful. And if we help them, we cannot fail to destroy the Stunted Men."

Hareton stood there, dreamily, for a moment. Then he said, "Half of us will stay to keep watch over the camp. The rest will accompany the Goura-Zannkas. Is that all right with all of you?"

"We accept."

"Then, all that remains is to pick the men."

"Let a toss of the coin decide," Guthrie said. "Except for myself, who must walk with them," he added with a hearty laugh.

"Why?"

"Because they wish it so."

"It's true," Hareton said.

The Blue-Eagle looked with awe at the giant.

The coin was flipped and Phillippe, Dick Nightingale, and Patrick Jefferson were chosen to go. Six blacks, in addition to Kouram, would accompany them.

When the Blue-Eagle knew that Guthrie would go on the expedition, he roared with joy. Turning to the men who had killed the prisoners, he proclaimed, "The Giant Phantom is with us!"

A great shout welcomed the news, and the Man-with-the-Horn-that-Made-Noise blew his instrument toward the horizons.

13.

The Battle of the Lake

Phillippe, Dick Nightingale, two blacks from the camp, and one hundred Goura-Zannkas were to explore the northwest shore and the islands. One of these was Humra, the runner with the ears of a jackal. None knew as well as he how to detect and interpret the most subtle sounds. When he lay against the ground, the earth revealed its mysteries. He could recognize from afar the heavy walk of the boar or the rumble of the rhinoceros. He did not confuse the step of the jackal with that of the leopard. He could discern the approach of the ostrich, the giraffe, even that of the python, long before they came into sight. And all cries and murmurs told him without fail the nature of their originators.

One of the sons of the Eagle was in command of the Goura-Zannka warriors. He was called Warzmao, the Python, because he could crawl like a reptile and could dive deep into the water.

They left before the rising of the moon, under a sky whitened by the stars. Soon, the warriors were following the contours of the shore. In the feeble starlight, the dark bodies seemed to be made out of pieces of night. Every now and then, Humra lay down close to the ground or Warzmao disappeared silently among the bushes. An hour went by without any clue to the presence of the Stunted Men. And yet they knew that they were being followed. Perhaps they had retreated into the desert? Or were they setting up ambushes?

Phillippe strained to hear and to see. His hearing was as

fine as, perhaps even finer, than Humra's, but he was a novice in the mysteries of the African night.

"This is a damned mess," whispered Dick Nightingale. "How can they fight in the dark? They won't manage to find more than one or two of the lice at any given time, and they prefer to die rather than talk."

Dick was brave, but he liked to talk too much. Phillippe said, "You'd better remain silent."

"Damn it," the man said. "I defy a wolf to hear me six yards away. And we are surrounded by these blacks."

It was true. The Python was keeping a cordon of Goura-Zannkas around the whites and their black auxiliaries. He did not want to expose them to a surprise attack, not because he valued their lives but because of their weapons.

"Let's stop talking anyway," Phillippe insisted. "And don't worry, Dick. I don't believe that the Goura-Zannkas want to fight in the dark. No more than the Stunted Men, anyway. You can be certain that they are not on the move without reason."

Dick remained silent, and the expedition carried on its monotonous search. The ground was thoroughly examined everywhere, and Humra kept listening to find out if any sound was coming from the depths of the earth. The solitude was not silent. They could hear intermittently the yap of a jackal, roars, the scream of the herbivores seized by the carnivores, the plaintive cry of the frogs among the reeds and the water-lilies. All things were mysterious, fascinating and terrible. Uncertain conqueror, man still possessed only a very small part of the savage land. In this thick darkness, he was lost in the midst of unvanquished night.

Phillippe's heart beat sharply, almost unbearably, but not because of fear. His only thought was for Muriel. He could almost see her in the phosphorescence of the lake and in the dusty brightness of the stars.

"The moon is rising," Dick Nightingale said harshly.

Red as a poppy flower, still half-dark, but growing brighter by the minute, the moon traced a river of light over the surface of the lake. The frogs welcomed it with a plaintive chant.

The vanguard of the Goura-Zannkas stopped. The scouts rejoined the main body, and suddenly a hundred voices howled a war-cry. For about five minutes, a confusing flight of projectiles was the only evidence of the enemy's presence. Those from the reeds and the bushes were aimed at the Goura-Zannkas, who replied by bombarding the vegetation with their spears.

"Are the Stunted Men really there?" Dick said, shaking his fist with frustration.

It was as yet only an imitation battle. Because of the distance of the enemy, the projectiles were harmless. The ambush of the Stunted Men had failed. They had planned to surprise the Men-of-the-Stars with an unforeseen attack, but the scouts had foiled their plan. Now, the Stunted Men were hesitant; the spear-points were, on both sides, dipped in a very strong poison. Before managing to reach the enemy, the attackers would lose a distressing number of men.

Warzmao, well aware of this, kept a sharp eye toward the papyrus reeds. The Stunted Men remained invisible, some of them hidden in the vegetation, the others concealed by irregularities in the rocks.

On both sides, patience was of equal intensity, but so was hatred, a hatred without limits. Its origin was lost in the night of the two races. If the Goura-Zannkas, more impetuous, had not thus far attacked in large numbers, it was because they knew that they were outnumbered and that their adversaries held a very strong position. Moreover, the Stunted Men had a flotilla of canoes on the lake to which they could retreat. The scouts had reported this.

"This might last a month," Dick Nightingale said. "These savages, sir, are a bunch of damned cowards."

"I don't believe so," Phillippe said. "Both races are very courageous. Don't underestimate a savage just because he is a savage."

But, in actuality, he was as impatient as Dick. He had positioned his small troop in the shelter of a hillock. If the Stunted Men attempted a massive assault, the black gun-bearers were to fire without stopping. They were poor shots, and Dick was cursed with bad eyesight. Phillippe told himself that he should have remembered that and so refused to take Dick along.

"Are our men marching out?" Dick asked loudly.

Approximately thirty Goura-Zannkas were moving forward in tight ranks, heading for the shore. They were shouting insults at the Stunted Men. They gave the impression that they intended to charge. A cloud of missiles rose from the papyrus reeds but the troop had stopped well out of range. The trick was evident; Warzmao wanted to tempt the adversary with the bait of an easy victory. To increase temptation, he had the rest of his warriors retreat.

"Look out!" Phillippe said. "Be ready to fire."

"They won't come out," Dick said. "They are rabbit warriors."

But Phillippe was giving precise instructions to his gun-bearers.

The Goura-Zannkas were still defying the enemy. The front runners were now completely exposed. At least seven hundred paces separated them from the main body of the expedition, and the shape of the lakeshore allowed the Stunted Men to attack head-on as well as from the flank. Furthermore, since they were numerically superior to the Goura-Zannkas, their chances of winning were great.

Phillippe's heart was beating fiercely. It seemed to him that the determination of the Stunted Men would decide Muriel's fate. Not to mention his fate and that of those with him.

No movement could be seen among the reeds, the grasses and the rocks. However, the harsh voices of the Stunted Men answered the loud clamors of the Men-of-the-Stars. Then, there was a brief silence. Out on the lake, a flotilla of canoes was moving about, then it started to come nearer. For a moment, a chain of rocks hid it from sight.

"Reinforcements," Dick said. "Things could get hotter!"

Warzmao was standing on a knoll. Doubtless, he was hesitating; the position of the forward group was fast becoming critical. He did not have time to sound a retreat. Frightening howls announced a coming attack. It began suddenly, lightning-like and frantic. Two groups, comprised of at least eighty men each, were coming up in bunches. The flank group was evidently trying to cut off the retreat of the Goura-Zannkas.

"Fire!" Phillippe screamed.

The massive body of the flank group was torn apart. Phillippe aimed at the first wave. Within a minute, he shot down seven or eight men.

Through an oversight of their scouts, the Stunted Men were unaware of the presence of the whites. The precautions insisted upon by Warzmao had fooled them. As brave as bulldogs when facing familiar weapons, even though they might be poisoned, they were confused by the presence of the thunder machines. Many among them remembered the fight in the forest where, in an instant, the Stunted Men had been faced with an extraordinary defeat. The defenders were admirably positioned, and the Stunted Men were dropping in bunches.

The troop on the left wailed mournfully. The Goura-Zannkas in the forefront fell upon the right-hand column, which was much less exposed to the gunfire than the left. Warzmao and his men were coming up at full speed. The Stunted Men began to mill around in bewilderment. Like the Athenians at Cheronea, they knew the despair of defeat and let themselves be killed without resistance. The clubs of the Goura-Zannkas were knocking them down by the dozen, while the gunfire of Phillippe and his men continued to pick off those near the edge of the battle.

Soon, the Goura-Zannkas and Stunted Men were so mixed that everyone except Phillippe stopped firing. He was a good enough shot to be sure of hitting individual targets, even in the moonlight. A few Stunted Men attempted a last-ditch resistance, but a ferocious assault crushed them. Then furious massacre followed, a primitive slaying, where the vanquished yields to the mysterious destiny of battles and, awaiting death, no longer attempts to revolt against it.

A hundred Stunted Men must have perished on the shore of that savage lake. Some survivors hid in the brush; others jumped into a dozen canoes tied up on the shore and headed out across the waters.

Other canoes were found, numbering a dozen, able to

carry ten men each. Warzmao decided to clean up the islands that could be seen offshore and to which, without doubt, the enemy was fleeing.

One of the canoes contained Phillippe, Dick Nightingale, and the gun-bearers.

14.

In the Bowels of the Earth

Stunted Men had been spotted getting off the canoes on the most northerly island. Phillippe landed there with his men. Presently, they were joined by the Goura-Zannkas who had swum after them, holding their spears in one hand. The canoe of the Stunted Men, hidden in a cove, proved that the enemy were still on the island. It was mainly rock with a few patches of grass mixed with lichen. A few clumps of papyrus reeds grew near the water. With Dick and six men dressed in the spear-proof overcoats, Phillippe set out to reconnoiter. But they found no Stunted Men.

When the small troop came back to the harbor, the oldest of the Goura-Zannkas spoke to Kouram, using sign language. Three times he pointed to the center of the island.

"That is where they vanished," Kouram said.

"Nobody can be hiding out there," Phillippe said. "You saw that as well as I, Kouram. If that is truly the place where they vanished, they can't be *on* the ground."

"They are *under* the ground, master."

He made a sign toward the Goura-Zannka, who gravely nodded his head.

"How does he know that?" Phillippe said.

Kouram attempted in vain to translate. But the old chief perceived that the phantom-man wanted to see for himself. He gave a brief order, and the Goura-Zannkas headed warily for the rock. Phillippe followed with Dick and his gun-bearers.

When they reached the spot, the Goura-Zannka chief called one of his men. The two rolled aside a rock over a crescent-shaped break in the surface. Phillippe saw a dark hole which led down below the earth. The old warrior spread his arms and said a few words in a grave tone. Undoubtedly, he was warning them.

Phillippe, Kouram and Dick looked at one another.

"What will the Goura-Zannkas do now?" Phillippe asked.

The chief seemed to understand. He pointed to Phillippe, Dick, Kouram, and the gun-bearers wearing the protective clothing, then to his warriors. Then he made gestures indicating that they would follow.

"Master," Kouram said, "he wants us to go ahead first. They think we are indestructible."

"We almost are," Nightingale said. He laughed. "Or else he trusts our weapons."

"We will walk in front," Phillippe said. "We must set them a good example."

Dick shrugged his shoulders. He was a fatalist whose bravery knew almost no limits.

"Are our gun-bearers ready?" Phillippe asked Kouram.

"They will follow you."

Phillippe turned and looked at them. Obviously, they had great faith. Having witnessed the victories of the whites, they thought them invincible.

"Forward," Phillippe said. He checked the free movement of his hunting knife in its sheath and then his gun.

The hole was rather steep but negotiable. Phillippe's electric lamp shot a violet cone into the darkness. After three minutes, they stopped. They found themselves in an almost horizontal corridor, the floor of which was full of holes. Half-seen beasts fled. The silence was deep.

Phillippe, turning around, saw in the subdued light faintly outlined heads and scintillating eyes. A few Goura-Zannka warriors were bending down or putting their ears close to the walls. Others were on the floor.

"Well?" Phillippe said.

"They came this way," Kouram said. "But we can hear nothing. Perhaps they have fled? Or perhaps they are still waiting for us? And who can know if they are not waiting in ambush in another cave?"

Phillippe gazed at the mysterious half-light. His lamp flashed on quartz and gemlike mineral. But there was nothing to show that men had passed this way.

"Let's move on."

Warzmao said something to his men. Two Men-of-the-Stars, evidently experts at reading tracks, had taken the lead. They were walking slowly, listening carefully, but nothing could be seen except for the stone walls. Only the stealthy steps of the warriors could be heard.

Presently, lights seemed to shine from the vault above. They entered a great natural hall, almost hexagonal in shape. The lights that shone on the ground were reflections from large rock-crystal blocks.

"These blocks almost seem to have been polished," Dick Nightingale said.

They could see a series of holes each of which was an entrance to passageways of varying widths. Phillippe counted ten of these, then turned anxiously toward the Goura-Zannkas.

The chief shook his head, but he did not seem surprised. He made Kouram understand that he had expected something of the sort. No doubt this was on account of the tales told by his ancestors. Evidently, neither he nor any of his warriors had ever come this far. Men of the light, inhabitants of the trees, they dreaded to enter the bowels of the earth.

"What should we do?" Phillippe said.

"It's worse than a labyrinth," Dick growled. "Even before we manage to inspect a few of these damned holes, the Stunted Men will be far away. Not counting the traps . . . the ambushes. . . ."

Phillippe suddenly felt tremendously discouraged. All that he had hoped for now appeared impossible to accomplish. And what proof was there that Muriel was in these caves? And why should she still be alive? No matter! They must go on!

He said to Kouram, "If the Goura-Zannkas will keep watch in this hall, we'll explore the exits."

"That will be very dangerous, master."

"No more than what we've already accomplished."

"Much more dangerous. We will face every trap set by the Stunted Men. They are the lords of the underworld."

"We'll have to take our chances."

Kouram lowered his head fatalistically. "It shall be as you wish, master."

"We will take half of our gun-bearers with us. The rest will stay to inspire confidence among the Goura-Zannkas. Dick, you will take command here."

"I would have preferred to go along with you," Nightingale said.

"If the Goura-Zannkas see only blacks, they will lose their confidence, and they will go back."

"Very well," Dick said. "But I don't like it."

Kouram succeeded in making the Goura-Zannkas understand Phillippe's aims because the black chieftain had had the same idea. He offered two of his best scouts to help in the search.

There was really no reason to choose one hole before the others. Phillippe entered a gallery picked at random, followed by Kouram and his small troop. That corridor, low and narrow, proved to be impassable.

"The Stunted Men never came this way, or else the rocks hold secrets for us," Kouram said, when they were stopped by the narrowness of the crevice.

"Let's go back," Phillippe said, after having felt the walls.

The second hole ended in a deadend. The third opened onto an enclosed grotto that resembled a savage temple because of its stalactites and stalagmites. But the fourth led to a spacious gallery which, after ten minutes' walk, still seemed endless.

"The Stunted Men came this way," Kouram said.

A Goura-Zannka scout touched Kouram on the shoulder. He turned. The man showed him the palm of his hand.

"Blood! It's blood, master," Kouram said.

The Goura-Zannka gestured for him to follow. Close to the wall, there was a purplish trail.

15.

The Underground Waters

The Goura-Zannka scout was walking briskly, certain now of the recent presence of his enemies. The small troop followed the purple rays of the electric light in the darkness.

After a few minutes of rapid travel, they came to a ninety-degree turn. At the same time, the vault came down and the walls closed in. Soon, the Goura-Zannka cried out. Kouram, close behind him, raised his arms. He did not have to give an explanation. The lamplight shone brightly on it.

"Water!" Phillippe said, his voice heavy with despair.

Kouram touched his arm. "A canoe, master."

It was on the stone floor just by the edge of the lake. Over the dim body of water was a vault rich in crystals, reflecting the light of the electric lamp. The waters nearby shone with hues of diamonds, sapphires, rubies and topaz.

Phillippe inspected the canoe. Why had the Stunted Men abandoned it there? Shouldn't they fear a trap? The craft, rather long, quite narrow, seemed to be fragile. It did hold two paddles, but there was only room for six men. Should they risk floating on these mysterious waters, in the night of the underworld, among men used to the life of moles? It would be folly and would almost surely end in disaster. But the fever of adventure and a strange exaltation had taken hold of Phillippe.

"Are there five men who will come with me?"

"Master, it means certain death."

Phillippe hesitated for a moment more, even though he was in the grip of madness.

"Kouram, we will take four gun-bearers; the rest will re-join the Goura-Zannkas."

Kouram did not argue. He had said what must be said. "Very well."

He picked out four gun-bearers. They did not object. They had a fatalistic confidence in the white man. Also, they may have felt easier being with Phillippe than with the warriors of Warzmao.

Phillippe said, "The canoe is in perfect condition. Let's get on board."

A few minutes later, the canoe was moving rapidly on the lake's surface. Kouram was paddling like a man from the South Seas. Phillippe, who had manned canoes in Canada, sat behind Kouram, paddling in rhythm with the black.

The crossing took close to an hour. Then, a flat, gray shore with a low vault over it appeared. Something sinister, foreboding, seemed to emanate from both the lake and the shore. The darkness, the silence, the vastness of the cave depressed them. They were glad to reach the other side. The shore did little to raise their spirits, however. To the right and left was nothing but a granite wall. Once more, they came upon a corridor. Before entering it, Phillippe stopped. No logic guided him; this underground foray was against all reason. If it were not for Muriel, he would never have come this far. They would have to catch up with the fleeing Stunted Men rapidly and take them by surprise. But the latter had the advantage, and no doubt their superior numbers would permit them to pick the best moment for an ambush.

He thought of Muriel and forced himself to move on. Despite his resolve, he did not walk swiftly. Then he slowed down even more. The passage had become very narrow, so that it would have been impossible to walk two abreast.

Suddenly, Kouram who had gone on ahead, stopped in his tracks. They had reached a turn in the corridor. A light seemed to come through the granite wall.

"See, master!"

Phillippe was already running forward. Both simultaneously reached the spot from which the light shone.

Through an oval opening, an irregularly shaped natural window too narrow to admit him, he could see a grotto. It was faintly lit, and a vague female shape was seated in the middle of the grotto. As his eyes became more adjusted to the darkness, he saw that she was not a black woman nor of the race of Stunted Men. She was a white woman, adorned with the golden hair of a legendary princess.

"Muriel!" he cried out.

He could not keep from shouting. The young girl shuddered and raised her head. Her great turquoise eyes gazed intently at the round opening.

"Who is calling me?" she said slowly, unbelievingly.

"C'est moi, Phillippe!"

In two leaps, she had reached the opening.

"You! You!" she said, and moaned.

By the lamplight, she looked pale, lean, haggard. It was as if she had suffered a year in a few hours.

"My father?" she said. "And all of you?"

"Safe and sound. But you, Muriel?"

"Oh! Take care! They're watching you. They are following you. They hope to trap you. My God! They're probably behind you now!"

"But what about you?"

She grimaced in the pale blue light. Phillippe could not tell if she was smiling or expressing revulsion.

"They haven't harmed me *yet.* Their acts are incomprehensible. I am at the mercy of their sorcerers. At times, they seem to be worshipping me. At other times, they become menacing. I don't know. I expect something horrible to happen."

She brushed her hand over her forehead. Her pupils were dilated. "You must run," she murmured. "They are the masters of these subterranean passages. They know you are here . . . run!"

"And leave you here?" Phillippe said. "No. We'll get you out of this!"

"How could you?" she said. "This grotto does not communicate with any other."

"Where does the light come from?"

"From above, from the sky. The cave opens onto a volcanic isle in the middle of the lake. Ah! Wait!"

Again she brushed her hand over her forehead as if she were trying to brush away a nightmare.

"Go on!"

"I can't. Go back where you came from. It's your only chance to save yourself."

"Muriel, I beg you."

"You must not risk your life needlessly!"

"We won't go back. I want to free you or die here. Tell me, Muriel."

"I must not!"

"I swear that we won't abandon you."

"My God," she sighed. "Very well. I think that your underground passage communicates with this isle. But you won't be able to reach it. *They* are already there."

A growl interrupted her. Three shadows had suddenly appeared behind her.

Phillippe's first reaction was to reach for his gun, but the Stunted Men had already reached Muriel. They surrounded her and dragged her away. He hesitated. It was impossible to aim accurately. They were standing too close together.

A moment later Muriel had disappeared, and the cave was empty. All that remained was his hope of reaching the rocky island mentioned by the young girl.

"Let's go!" Phillippe shouted as he ran down the corridor.

Kouram and the gun-bearers followed him.

After ten minutes, they saw ahead of them a steadily increasing glow. A rather steep incline rose before the small troop. They climbed it swiftly and found themselves out in the open air. They were in a rocky circle with jagged edges; above them was the moon. Through a break in the rock, the lake shuddered with the reflected images of the constellations.

"There they are!" Kouram shouted.

A canoe was leaving the shore. In it was Muriel and five Stunted Men. This time, Phillippe, persuaded that the

"They surrounded her and dragged her away."

young girl would be lost forever if he did not rescue her now, took aim with his rifle. A shot rang out; a Stunted Man whirled and dropped his paddle. The remaining four howled frenetically. The gun thundered a second time, and the top of a man's head disappeared. The survivors started paddling furiously. Phillippe shot down two more men. The last one threw himself upon Muriel.

The savage head and that of the young girl were so close together that the slightest deviation in aim might be fatal. At times, both were in the line of fire. Phillippe, his hands shaking slightly, waited for the right moment.

The man who had grabbed Muriel was now trying to throw her into the lake. Screaming, she struggled with him. For an instant, she managed to push the brute away from her. For about six seconds, they were separated. Between them was a space of about three decimeters. Both were standing up now. The Stunted Man growled and lifted a hand. Phillippe forced his hands to stop trembling and squeezed the trigger. The man toppled overboard without upsetting the canoe.

The blacks howled with enthusiasm.

Muriel had grabbed one of the paddles and was coming back to the isle. Phillippe was shaking from head to foot. When the young girl reached the shore, tears were streaming down his cheeks. Muriel ran to him and threw her arms around him.

"Oh!" she murmured. "It's as if the world had just been born."

He kissed her again and again until she pushed him away, but she was smiling. Then, raising her joined hands, she said, "From the depths I cried out to You . . . and I have been answered."

Then she said to Phillippe, "After my father, you are the one who has given me my life."

"Oh! Muriel," he said softly, "I think I would have died if you had been carried off."

They stood for an instant in silence. All sorts of pictures rose tumultuously in their minds, bright images. Then Muriel said, "We must leave this place. They can come out of the earth at any time. I don't know by what miracle you managed to get through the tunnels or why I was left unguarded for a little while."

She looked at the harbor where she had come ashore and said, "Yesterday, there were more than thirty canoes here. Where are they now? Something out of the ordinary must have happened."

"We attacked them, aided by the Goura-Zannkas, and we managed to overwhelm them."

"The Goura-Zannkas?"

"Blacks who are now our allies." He went on, "However, many Stunted Men managed to flee. Perhaps they are fighting elsewhere."

"And my father?"

"He's back at the camp."

"We must hurry, Phillippe."

"We left Dick Nightingale and a bunch of men back in the tunnel. They are waiting for us."

"We must not go back the same way you came!"

"But then how . . . ?"

"Head toward the lakeshore. Then warn your friends."

"I only hope that they weren't surprised by the Stunted Men."

"Where did you go underground?"

"By an isle in the north. A rock hid the entrance."

"I know that isle. Have they all gone underground?" Muriel wondered.

The canoe was roomy enough to hold all of them. For a quarter of an hour they paddled over the water in silence. The lake was alive with submarine life. Here and there, huge scaly backs briefly arose or the moon gleamed on long teeth momentarily breaking the surface. How had the blacks who had swum to the isle managed to get by them? Perhaps the uproar had frightened the monsters.

After a short hesitation, Phillippe directed the craft toward the northern island. If the Goura-Zannkas and the canoes could be found there, it would be a tremendous help. Perhaps, after all, the Stunted Men had given up the fight. Their defeat had been a crushing one. Like most savages, they would take their time before seeking revenge.

One of the blacks shouted. He pointed toward the northeast where there was a dark cloud of canoes. The Stunted Men!

Phillippe ground his teeth. The northern island was more than a kilometer away. Would the oncoming men have time to block their passage?

"Hurry up!" he yelled.

That order was not necessary. The rowers understood their danger. They put their backs, their souls, into their labor. For two minutes, it was impossible to evaluate the chances of the adversaries. The canoes of the Stunted Men were moving forward with the best speed allowed by the imperfect construction of their crafts and their paddling. Two of their canoes were well ahead of the others.

"Don't shoot, anyone!" Phillippe ordered.

Their ammunition supply was low. Sure of his skill, Phillippe wanted the bullets for himself.

"Is your gun fully loaded, Kouram?"

Kouram nodded. The two canoes were getting within spear range. Slowly, Phillippe aimed. He fired.

"One less to worry about," Kouram growled.

The blacks began to laugh as Phillippe picked a new victim. A second later, another Stunted Man dropped his paddle. Almost simultaneously, furious shouting sounded on the island. Warzmao's tall silhouette appeared on the red rock.

Disheartened, the Stunted Men gave up the fight. The two head canoes rejoined the rest of the flotilla, and it disappeared over the starlit waters.

The group rejoined the warriors on the island. Their ranks had swelled with the arrival of reinforcements brought by Warzmao. Those who were still underground were sent for.

"This time, I think we are safe," Kouram said.

Phillippe thought so too. Once they reached the shore where the rest of the Goura-Zannkas were and once the expedition had returned from the caves, the Stunted Men would almost surely give up. For the time being, anyway.

"I only hope that nothing has happened to Dick," Phillippe thought.

But that worry also vanished. Dick and his companions emerged from the red rock.

Warzmao and his warriors gazed with an almost mystical adoration upon the girl that the Phantom-Chief had rescued from the bowels of the earth. Their faith in the invincible power of the whites was justified. Only gods, or men like gods, could go down into the dark underground of the Stunted Men and emerge unharmed and victorious. Or wrest from the Stunted Men the golden-haired woman.

Landing on the mainland shore, they met the main body of the Goura-Zannkas. No alarm having disturbed them, they had assembled the wounded and the prisoners. These numbered more than fifty.

"It will be a great feast," Kouram said.

"It's awful," Muriel said. "Can't we stop them?"

"By Jupiter," Dick growled. "It's not important. If we interfere, they might turn on us."

The warriors of Warzmao left for the forest of their birth, the captives closely guarded by spearmen. The wounded were carried on shields or on crossed branches. Thus must the ancestors of the Goura-Zannkas have behaved in the days when the kings of Assyria "flayed like trees" their vanquished enemies.

Nothing had really changed since those days of long ago, and, no doubt, since the dawn of sentence in man. The Goura-Zannkas had the same weapons, the same tools, the same rites and the same enemies. How many times, in the martial night, had Stunted Men been brought like these to serve as food? How many times had the Goura-Zannkas, vanquished in battle, been mutilated and tortured by the stunted victors?

"Yes," Phillippe murmured, thinking of all these things. "This is a scene from olden times."

He was walking alongside Muriel, deep in thought, and sometimes their eyes would meet in a profound softness.

"These things will all end someday," she said.

"No doubt. But perhaps with the disappearance of the Goura-Zannkas and the Stunted Men, felled by bullets, the

bombs or the plague of white men . . . you see, Muriel, our
civilization is the most homicidal that has ever existed. For
three centuries, we have exterminated more peoples and
tribes than all the conquerors of antiquity and the Middle
Ages have. The slaughter and devastation wrought by the
ancient Romans was child's play compared to ours. Do you
not live, Muriel, in a land larger than Europe, where you
have destroyed the red race?"

The young girl only sighed. An image of her father appeared before her eyes, so clear and yet so soft, that she
held out her arms avidly, as if to embrace him.

"Are we still very far from the camp?"

"Perhaps two hours."

"And if it has been attacked during your absence?" she
added.

"That's almost impossible. Isn't it, Kouram?"

"Yes, master. The Stunted Men who attacked on the
lakeshore were as numerous as two clans. That almost
never happens. The Blue-Eagle is back there with more
warriors than Warzmao had. And against the elephant gun,
the rifles, and the machine gun, what could the Stunted
Men accomplish?"

These words reassured Muriel somewhat. And then she
told about her captivity.

The daily life of the Stunted Men was almost animal-
like. They slept much, even during the day, but once they
got moving they could walk without rest and in darkness.
They had never given up the pursuit of the white man's
caravan. Their sorcerers practiced mysterious sacrifices, for
which warriors were chosen at random. These drank a liquid prepared from plant juices and then fell asleep. The
veins of their necks were slashed open. Their blood was
gathered by the chiefs. If the victims did not succumb, their
lives were spared.

"I still don't know why they spared me," Muriel said.
"It seemed that I was a sort of good-luck charm for
them to give them victory over their enemies."

A blood-colored moon grew larger as it prepared to
drop below the horizon. Jackals were watching them; their
narrow heads and sharp ears were profiled for a moment

and then vanished in the shadows. A lion, crouched on a knoll, roared. A moment later, he had disappeared.

"We are getting close," Phillippe said.

Muriel was exhausted, but that part of the forest where men lived in trees was in sight.

Suddenly, the column stopped. The front-runners were falling back to the center. Scouts came running up.

"Is it still those vermin?" Nightingale cried.

Kouram was exchanging signs with Warzmao. The young chief was standing on a mound looking into the darkness.

"What is it?" Phillippe asked.

"They are not Stunted Men," Kouram said. "They are other enemies of the Blue-Eagle, true men. They learned that Warzmao had with him only a part of the Men-of-the-Stars while the Blue-Eagle is off with another part. They must want revenge, master, and they will try to get it while the Men-of-the-Stars are weak."

"I thought that half that clan had perished."

"Warzmao did not take with him half the Men-of-the-Stars, and he brings back even less."

"Is the road blocked?"

"Yes, master, as far as the lake."

Phillippe climbed up on the hillock. The moon had just sunk out of sight. He could see nothing but the hazy shapes of the vegetation. Even the Goura-Zannkas were hiding in the tall grass or in the hollows of the ground.

"Damn it," Nightingale growled. "This country is terribly inhospitable. I wish I could get some sleep."

"Perhaps you will be able to do so," Kouram said, gravely. "Warzmao will wait for daylight before starting again."

"And if these sons of bitches should attack?"

"We'll wake you up."

Here and there a dark body was crawling among the graminous plants. Warzmao was stationing his sentries. A complete silence fell heavily on the solitude. The great carnivores had stopped hunting.

Muriel and Phillippe sat down on the ground. The breeze seemed to come down from the stars. And from this threatening night, when beasts and men had exterminated each other, this night full of menace and horror, emanated a peace so soft that the two young people almost forgot the savage law of the world around them.

It was the time of dawn. The fleeting tropical sunrise had scarcely brought enchantment to the lake before the red furnace of the sun, appearing between two hills, began to burn it away.

"Are they attacking?" Dick Nightingale stammered, having just awakened with a start.

"No," Kouram said. "They have come a little closer. They block our way completely. We must disperse them or else retreat."

"How many are they?"

"I do not know, master. Warzmao has shown two times ten times the fingers of his hands."

"Then that would be two hundred?"

"How could he have counted them?" Dick said sullenly.

"He did not count them, I suppose," Phillippe said. "But he evaluates their number by deducting the dead, the wounded, and the captives."

"Dead also," Dick said, "since they have been eaten."

"Warzmao must still have between seventy and seventy-five men who are in good shape. You, master, Mr. Nightingale, and the gun-bearers must be worth at least a hundred men."

"Much more," Dick said forcefully.

"But how can we attack?" the black said. "They will retreat, remaining out of sight as far as the river, harassing us all the way. Then we will have to cross, and they will be able to hide in the reeds and hurl their spears at us from close range."

"For the moment," Phillippe said, "there's little we can do."

The pink sun, still half-hidden, was rising rapidly above the lake, emanating its beneficial yet destructive energy. Phillippe, Warzmao, Dick and Kouram were scanning the territory around them. But there was nothing to be seen.

After awhile, two woolly heads appeared furtively at the crest of a mound. Reassured by the distance—more than three hundred yards—the two warriors rose. They were both tall men. The tallest brandished a spear and shouted something.

"He is defying the Goura-Zannkas," Dick said.

"That's the chief," Kouram replied, after having exchanged signs with Warzmao. "If you could hit him, master, the warriors will be scared off."

Phillippe had taken aim, but he hesitated. He did not have any reason, so far, to hate the black stranger.

He decided to only wound him, but realizing that prestige had to be maintained he told Kouram, "I will hit him in the shoulder. Try to make Warzmao understand that it's a warning for the enemy."

Kouram, disappointed, gestured at great length. Warzmao failed to understand, but he howled, "The life of the Red-Rhinoceros is in the hands of our allies Their chief will be wounded!"

At these words, the gist of which was understood by the whites and Kouram, the enemy chief burst out laughing. He never finished his laugh. Phillippe fired. The tall Negro, hit in the shoulder, promptly dropped his spear.

"The allies of the Goura-Zannkas are infallible and their arms have the power of thunder," Warzmao shouted. "If the Gou-Anndas retreat, their lives will be spared."

The enemy chief and his companion disappeared. There was a long silence. Here and there a dark body crawled through the tall grass. Then, whistling sounds were heard, answering one another from the lake to the baobabs that were on the edge of the forest.

Finally, three runners came up and stopped in front of Warzmao to speak to him. He laughed and then signalled Kouram that the enemy was hastily retreating. The frontrunners of the Goura-Zannkas were following them.

"And what if it's a trap?" Phillippe said, looking at Muriel.

"We are preceded by invisible scouts," Kouram answered. "At the first sign of danger, the warriors will stop."

Phillippe gave the order for the departure, but he did not feel at ease. The retreat of the Gou-Anndas could end in ambush. They moved slowly and the column stopped often.

"The warriors are still there," Dick said.

After an hour's march, there was an alert. The warriors were holding their spears at the ready. All felt that the enemy was planning a surprise for them. Soon it became a certainty. The Goura-Zannkas were surrounded!

Phillippe cursed, but he gave the order to march forward. They proceeded slowly, alert, protected by a circle of scouts.

Suddenly, savage cries arose.

"The attack!" Dick Nightingale yelled, ready to fire.

The cries had stopped. A stormy atmosphere enveloped them. Then, far away, a horn blew. An enormous clamor arose. Everywhere around the column the scouts were straightening up from their crouch.

"What is it?" Phillippe cried.

Warzmao was uttering the victory cry.

"It's the main body of the Goura-Zannkas," Kouram said. "We are safe."

Phillippe smiled with joy. They had been delivered! Muriel was no longer in danger. The Gou-Anndas were fleeing from their cover, completely bewildered. A group of Goura-Zannkas pursued them with spears just as the front-runners of the Blue-Eagle appeared.

Muriel cried out loudly and stretched her arms toward the west. Ironcastle was coming with Sir George and the colossal Guthrie.

16.

Life and Death

At the hour when the shadows lengthen, in the sacred clearing, the Goura-Zannkas were gathering for the evening feast. Twenty Stunted Men and as many Gou-Anndas were immersed in the lake to make their flesh more tender and to give it more flavor. The fires were ready.

It was a day of supreme victory. The Goura-Zannkas, in less than a month, had triumphed over the sons of the Red-Rhinoceros, the sons of the Black-Lion, and also over their thousand-year enemies, the Stunted Men, masters of the caves and the tunnels.

The Blue-Eagle marched toward the camp of the chiefs of the Faces-without-Color. There also fires were lit against the perilous shadows of night. The Blue-Eagle gazed with admiration upon the immense Guthrie, and he looked at Ironcastle gravely.

While he repeated his own words with gestures, he proclaimed, "This night will be the greatest night of the Goura-Zannkas since Zauma made himself Master of the Forest. Twenty Stunted Men and twenty Gou-Anndas will give their strength and their courage to the Goura-Zannkas. Wammha would be proud to share the flesh of the vanquished with the great Phantom Chiefs since he is their friend. And he knows that they are the masters of death. The chief of wisdom, the giant chief, and the other chiefs who can strike farther than the voice of the Horn-of-Sound carries perhaps would like to take part in the great feast?"

Hareton understood only too well. He replied with words and gestures, "Our clans do not eat human flesh, and it is forbidden for them to see it being eaten."

118

The Blue-Eagle was astonished. He said, "How is that possible? What do you do with the vanquished? Your life must be very sad!"

Now he knew why their skins were so pale. The strange taboo against eating the flesh of their enemies had caused their skins to be bleached. He said, perhaps with a trace of irony, "Wammha will send to his friends some antelopes and wild boars."

Phillippe paid little attention to this. The green shadows, bathed by the shimmering reflections of the river, enhanced the brightness and grace of Muriel. This daughter of the Angels, glorious with hair woven from the sun and the moonlight, brought to mind blonde goddesses, mountain nymphs or water sprites rising from the mysterious lakes of the north. She drew around herself all the beautiful desires of man. She was a creature of enchantment.

Their eyes met, and he stammered, "Muriel . . . perhaps you know it . . . but without you, my future is nothing but darkness!"

She murmured, "I owe you my life."

"Then," he said, "if I had not come back there. . . ."

"Oh, Phillippe! No! You did not have to save my life to make me feel like this."

It seemed to him that creation itself had blown a new breath over him, over this forest. The river emerged from this dream garden where the world's first rivers had run, and the trees had just been born on an Earth that had only recently arisen above the waters.

He heard a shuffling in the grass. He turned. Ironcastle was approaching. His expression showed that he had overheard them.

He put his hand on Phillippe's shoulder. "You can confide in her, my son. Her heart is pure and her soul steadfast."

17.

The Plant Kingdom

"What a strange world!" Guthrie said.

The expedition was moving slowly over a blue and purple savanna. Tall and sturdy, the grass rustled harmoniously, sounding almost like the indistinct voice of violins. Here and there were clumps of palm trees with indigo leaves and banyans with amethyst-colored leaves. A yellow fog covering the sun harmonized with the weird hues of leaves and grass.

"We have entered the Domain of the Plants," Hareton said. "It's fantastic, incredible, unique. And," he paused, "unnatural."

He had ordered that the animals be restrained from eating the plants. But these orders were not necessary. The camels, goats, and asses had smelled the blue plants and the purplish grass, then turned away. The ape seemed worried; his round eyes moved from side to side as if he suspected an attack.

"The beasts will die of hunger," Sir George said.

"Not yet," Hareton said, pointing to the fodder loaded on the camels and asses.

"Yes, you had foreseen something like this," Guthrie said. "But at best, there is only enough to feed them through tomorrow morning."

"They are beasts of the desert. If we ration them, they won't suffer much, at least for several days."

Guthrie shrugged his shoulders carelessly.

A soft wind had begun to blow. From the plain arose weak voices, voices of tiny violins, of harps, evanescent voices of mandolins which formed a strange symphony, at once charming and indistinct.

"It sounds almost like a concert," Muriel said.

Whenever they neared an island of palm trees or banyans, the voices swelled slightly, just like muted organs.

The yellow fog, heaviest toward the west, seemed to form a plain of topaz hue beyond the amethyst-and-sapphire-colored plain. Here and there was a patch of purplish earth, gleaming metallically.

Flies of an enormous size, the largest as big as small birds, flew around them. Their reddish swarms followed the caravan and whirled around the animals, buzzing like beetles.

Many of them fell upon the camels and the donkeys. They scuttled over the animals with fantastic speed, but it was soon evident that they were harmless. Tiny birds scarcely larger than scarabs sprang from the grass, perched on stalks of gramineous plants, some chirping shrilly. The flies were pursuing them and, though less swift, they sometimes managed to grab a bird. They disappeared with their prey into the tall grass.

"It's awful!" Muriel cried, having just witnessed a fly grab a small bird.

Guthrie laughed and said, "It's about time they had their turn. Birds have been eating flies for a long time. It's better for us than if they were venomous."

The plain, shining and dreadful, still spread before them.

"We can put up with hunger for a long time," Sir George said. "But what about thirst?"

"A large river runs from east to west," Hareton answered. "We have to come across it. We will reach it during the night or tomorrow. Our gourds are more than half-full. We'll get by."

The caravan stopped at noon on one of the bands of red rock bare of all plants. The blacks busied themselves preparing the meal.

"On this barren rock, we can be certain we won't be breaking any of the unwritten laws of this land," Hareton said.

Thanks to the cloud that covered the sun, it was possible

to stand outside the tent. Both whites and blacks were subdued and worried-looking. This land seemed stranger than
anything they could imagine.

"Uncle Hareton," Guthrie said, after the meal had been
served, "if we can't eat the plants, what will become of us?
I feel that we are more in danger than when we were fighting the Stunted Men."

He swallowed a huge slice of smoked meat and laughed.
Nothing could take away his enjoyment of life for long.

"Don't worry so much," Hareton replied. "We'll find
some green plants. Or plants that will be half green and
half red. And our animals will graze. If all the plants are
inedible how can the animals of this land manage to live?
In the meantime, our camels, donkeys and goats can't eat a
single stalk of this immense feeding ground."

"Oh!" Muriel said.

Her outstretched hand was pointing to a strange creature
obviously observing them. It was a toad as large as a cat, a
hairy toad. It had golden scintillating eyes. The explorers
were even more fascinated by its third eye than by its size
and its fur. This eye was at the top of its skull and could
turn in any direction.

"Stupendous!" Phillippe said.

"Why?" Hareton said. "Is it not true that you can find a
scarcely developed eye, hidden it is true, in most reptiles?
It appears that this atrophied organ was functional in ancient reptiles, and batrachians are close kin to reptiles."

The toad suddenly leaped. A moment later, it had vanished through a crack in the rocky ground.

"There must surely be some water underground," Sir
George said. "Which would explain the dense growth of
those blue and purple plants."

The tiny birds flew by, their faint cries like fairy trum-
pets. One of them had dropped to the ground not far from
Muriel. Hypnotized by the presence of human beings, it
failed to hear a giant fly which suddenly fell upon it.

"Oh, no!" the young girl shouted, horrified.

She ran forward and scared off the insect. The small
bird, bleeding from one wing, chirped faintly. She took it
carefully in her hand.

In its tiny body, the bird had the beauty of the setting sun, the brightness of beryllium clouds, the colors of an amethyst and a topaz, with strains of purple running throughout. No butterfly had wings more finely hued, and the scarlet head, covered with bright green spots, appeared to be made of an unknown material.

"What embroiderer, what painter, what jeweler, could achieve a similar masterpiece in such a small space?" Hareton said.

"And nature lets this masterpiece be eaten by flies!" Phillippe said.

For the rest of the day, the caravan moved toward the southwest. The plain went on endlessly with its violet or blue grass, under the overhanging cloud of amber and gold, and so did the strange music of the wind-brushed plants.

"Frightfully monotonous," Guthrie said. "I'm getting fed up with blue and purple. They are making me sick."

"They *are* tiresome colors," Sir George said. "We should be wearing yellow or orange glasses."

"But I have some! And I had almost forgotten about them," Hareton said. "My only excuse is that everyone here has perfect eyesight. No one is myopic, no one is far-sighted."

"And no one is cross-eyed," Guthrie said, grinning.

Nightfall was not far away. Once more they set up camp on an isle of red soil.

"It's easy on the eyes," Phillippe said.

"Yes, but what about the river?" Sir George said. "I don't see any end to this plain, and by tomorrow evening our gourds will be empty."

"On top of that, the animals will be able to have only one more drink. And only half-rations at that!" Guthrie said.

"God will provide," Hareton said. "There must be some water under all this land." He pointed to two huge toads disappearing into a hole in the ground.

"Well, at best, a jackal might get through, but certainly not a man," Phillippe said.

"Especially not me," Guthrie said, grinning again.

They were men with brave hearts and confident souls. In

spite of the menacing alienness of the land, they enjoyed their evening meal. The blacks did not seem so relaxed; they muttered among themselves and started nervously at any unfamiliar sound.

Phillippe and Muriel had gone off together to the edge of the camp. Through the amber fog, a fabulous moon was rising like a vermilion-and-copper medal. Phillippe was intoxicated with both its beauty and Muriel's. In the bright face, reminding him of mother-of-pearl and April clouds, her eyes shone like jade. And her long hair shone like ripe wheat.

"We'll be glad once we've conquered these difficulties and have seen these strange lands," she said. "The future is now less frightful than it seemed back there when you were pursuing those monsters."

"How I would like to see you back in civilization. I need to know that you are safe, Muriel."

"Who knows?" she said dreamily. "Security does not really exist anywhere. This savage land may have saved us from worse danger. We are insignificant little things, Phillippe. The man who has escaped from lions may be killed by tripping over a rug."

Looking at her, touching her, he forgot all about dark threats. He tasted the sweetness of a magic moment. He would never forget it as long as he lived.

18.

The Water of Life

"The animals are thirsty," Guthrie said. "And so am I."

The travelers had drunk the last drops from the gourds. Now, in the plain without end, they were moving forward among violet plants, blue trees, and over scarlet earth. They were being held by the desert as if they were its prey and the sun, having beaten its way through the clouds, was trying to drink their blood. In spite of this, they had to move forward. The giant flies accompanied the music of the grass with their sinister buzzing. More and more it resembled the faint peal of distant bells. When the wind blew, they could hear the tink-tonking of alarm bells.

"I thought the river was much nearer," Hareton said.

"You really believe there *is* a river?" Sir George asked.

"I believe so, yes. Kouram swears there is one."

Sir George swept the horizon with his binoculars.

"Nothing!"

There were no more trees in sight. The grass was growing stiff and sturdy.

"There's water under the ground. Maybe *that's* where we ought to look for it," Phillippe said.

"We would lose much time," Ironcastle said. "I'm asking for a few more hours, that's all."

"Agreed, Uncle Hareton," Guthrie said. "But for how many days can we endure this thirst?"

"I don't know. Camels can hold out for a month, even longer . . . men, two days, three days, according to the humidity and the heat."

"The air is awfully dry. My tongue feels like leather,"

125

Guthrie growled. "I'm afraid I'll be the one who'll least be able to put up with this."

Gloominess enveloped the caravan. The sinking sun became gold-colored, then enlarged to a swollen orange. The end of the day was near.

The animals were suffering. The donkeys and the goats were staggering, the former silent, the latter bleating piteously. The blacks no longer talked, and they looked at the whites with questioning eyes. That great faith which the victories of the whites had created in them was withering away.

Hareton summoned Kouram. "What are the men saying?"

"They are afraid, master. This is a country of death. The grass is the enemy of the animals and us."

"Tell them not to be afraid, Kouram. We know where we are going."

Kouram's eyes lowered.

"Have we got much farther to go?" he asked. He shivered.

"Everything will change once we've reached the river."

"If *Doomballa* so wills," Kouram said. "But I will tell the men that you have promised that we will soon find water."

The sun was on the point of disappearing when the caravan reached a red isle. While they were getting ready to rest, they saw several giant frogs bouncing around and vanishing into holes in the ground.

"Where there are frogs, water is nearby," Muriel said.

"Then there must be an underwater lake here," Sir George said.

"Let's look," Guthrie said. "My thirst is becoming unbearable."

The goats were bleating plaintively and loudly, while the donkeys were smelling the ground impatiently.

Phillippe, Sir George and Sydney inspected the holes. These were narrow, showing no traces of humidity.

"We would have to dig," Phillippe said.

"That's what we'll do," Guthrie said. "Let's find some soft earth."

After a search covering several acres, they found a spot where they could work their way down into the ground. Guthrie went to get his drill. An hour's work with it resulted in a deep hole. They became excited when the earth suddenly became damp. But that wetness did not increase, and then it suddenly diminished.

"That's strange," Phillippe said. "Evidently, the wetness is caused by water seeping through from somewhere else. There has to be water nearby."

"Close by?" Hareton said. "If the water is only a hundred yards away, it might as well be twenty miles. We're too weak to keep up the digging, and the drill is almost out of gas."

Nevertheless, they scattered for an intensive search. And found no indication of water.

"It will be a sad night," Sydney said. "All we've managed to do is to get even more thirsty."

They slept badly, awaking before dawn. They felt that this was to be their last day on earth. The air, like a great invisible octopus, was drinking their bodies dry drop by drop.

"Let's not linger here," Guthrie said, plaintively. "We'll make better time during the night and in the early morning. If we last that long."

"It would be best if two of us went ahead to reconnoiter," Sir George suggested.

"I was thinking about it," Hareton said.

"Sir George and I!" Guthrie cried.

"It would be best if Sir George and Phillippe went," Hareton said.

"Why?"

"Because of your weight," Hareton said with a wan smile. "The safari can dispense with two camels for the explorers, although these are weak. But you're almost too heavy for even a strong camel."

"Very well," Guthrie said reluctantly.

Kouram chose two animals, the fleetest of the bunch, and their load was transferred to the other animals.

"They will be good guides," the black said. "They can smell water from far away."

Ten minutes later, the two men had left. The camels were moving rapidly, as if they understood that they were being taken to search for water.

The moon was becoming more and more orange as it fell in the west. Though enormous, its light decreased, while the constellations became brighter. A slight phosphorescence rose from the earth. The air was soft. The ringing of the plants seemed to announce some mystical ceremony in the depths of the savanna.

"It's as if we were on another planet," Sir George said softly. "Here I feel as if we had no past and no future."

"No," Phillippe said pensively. "We are far from the promised land."

The moon took on the color of virgin copper. The dawn came swiftly and was gone. And the fiery ball of the sun rose over the plain.

They scanned the horizon avidly. Nothing. Nothing but that interminable ocean of blue grass mixed with shades of indigo and purple. They pushed on, following the southwest direction recommended by Ironcastle.

"Frightful," Sir George said. "A wasteland of vegetation."

The tormenting, weakening thirst became worse as the fiery orb, rising, sucked the little water left in them.

Thirst! It corroded them as if they were made of soft iron. Phillippe, semiconscious, saw mirages which he half-believed were real: springs coming out of the earth with a lively murmur, an alcaraza in the shade of a patio, pitchers of lemonade covered with dew. . . .

Now and then, he said softly, "Fountains, rivers, lakes. . . ."

"Oh!" Sir George said with a melancholy smile. "I'm mostly reminded of a good tavern."

The camels were slowing down, and Phillippe's seemed ready to collapse.

"Hope they can hang on," he said.

"They will," Sir George croaked. "They know we are looking for water. They understand that it would be dangerous to stop."

The huge flies were buzzing frenetically around the men and beasts.

"It's a good thing they're not attacking us," Phillippe said in a creaking voice.

"I am beginning to think that we, as well as the camels, are poisonous to them."

"Then, why are they following us?"

"I hope it is because they are heading for water. If that's so, we're going in the right direction."

Silence fell once more, a particular silence that the sound of bells caused by the grass rendered fantastic. Nothing. Always the blue and violet stems of grass with, here and there, a sparse oasis of trees.

"I wonder what's becoming of them, back there," Phillippe murmured. In spite of his thirst, he was thinking about Muriel.

Sir George shook his head. He seemed impassive, but being from a humid climate, he suffered even more than Phillippe.

"If they must, they will drink the milk of two or three goats," he answered finally. "And then, there are the camels . . . a camel usually has water in its hump . . . and twenty gallons of blood!"

The Englishman looked at his mount. "As far as we are concerned, it's impossible," he said, sighing. "We *must* reach water!"

A long silence ensued. Images, now harsh, hard, and miserable, filled their minds. And the sun kept shining on them so powerfully that they felt as if their bone marrow was drying up.

Suddenly, a camel raised its head wearily and cried out. Its companion snorted. Both of them began to walk faster.

"What's the matter with them?" Phillippe rasped.

"I don't dare hope what I'm thinking," Sir George whispered.

The terrain was no longer flat. On a low hill, they saw grass and bushes that were *green* . . . both men looked at it, dazzled. The familiar color of the vegetation gladdened them.

And now, the camels were galloping as if they had gone

mad. They clambered, bellowing, up a hill and a harsh cry, a cry of thankfulness, burst from Phillippe's lips.

"Water! Water!"

And there it was, the sovereign mother, source of all that lives. It was there, the water of Genesis, the water without which all would die.

A large river . . . It flows on, wide and slow, enclosed in trees, reeds, and tall grass. It spreads a determined fecundity everywhere.

The camels forgot their weariness and galloped like pure-bred dromedaries. In five minutes, gasping, panting, they had reached the shore of the river and plunged their snouts into it. They drank as if they would never stop.

The men rolled off their mounts and into the water. There, half-submerged, they scooped handfuls of water into their mouths.

Finally, Sir George said, "We must stop for awhile. Or we'll die."

"But it's so delicious!" Phillippe said.

Sir George offered him a grayish mint. "Against microbes," he said. "Argh!" he cried out hoarsely, standing up and pointing to a small island, twenty yards from the shore. An extraordinary beast had appeared from amid the tall grass. It had the same shape as an ancient Egyptian crocodile, the long huge jaws, the monstrous teeth, the short legs and muscular tail—but in lieu of scales, long hair* grew on the body and skull. The eyes, unlike the glassy eyes of reptiles, shone like those of an angry leopard.

A third eye also shone at the top of its head.

"What kind of monster is that?" Phillippe said. "Even in prehistoric times, no saurian ever looked like it. But our knowledge of paleontology is limited, fragmentary."

The animal was eyeing them fixedly. The men grabbed their guns and waited for its next move.

A barking sound made them turn around. Its head thrown back, a blue antelope was running at full speed toward the river. The wild beast that was chasing it with thir-

* A reptile with hair seems fantastic. But refer to *Dinosaur Renaissance*, Robert T. Bakker, *Scientific American*, April, 1975.

ty-foot bounds was covered with tan hair, spotted here and there with pink. It was as huge as a Siberian tiger.

"It's a leopard," Sir George growled.

Distracted by this formidable beast, they did not notice the hairy crocodile plunge into the river.

"Watch out!" Sir George shouted.

The antelope and the leopard were running toward the promontory on which the men were standing. They retreated upstream, and the beasts reached the shore at the same time. The antelope was on the point of throwing itself into the river when it stopped abruptly, struck with stark fear.

At the point of the promontory, the hairy saurian had just emerged, its yellow eyes gazing at the fugitive beast. Paralyzed by terror, the antelope turned its finely shaped head upward. In its dark mind, pictures followed one another rapidly. Back where it had come from were tall grasses, the pleasure of moving around and of being alive . . . and over here, eternal night. . . .

The leopard pounced, and with a blow of its muscular paw, struck the antelope down. However, the hairy saurian was now attacking.

In spite of the danger, the two men were gripped by the same savage curiosity that had brought Romans to the circus.

"Two magnificent beasts," Sir George said as he examined his carbine.

The leopard, one paw resting on its gasping victim, was watching the reptile. It hesitated only a moment. Then opening its immense jaws, crouching on its short legs, it readied itself for the battle. It was three times as heavy as the feline. Its eyes were shining fiercely. The leopard roared. It was moving forward on a tangent, in an attempt to surprise the reptile and jump on its back. But the saurian had an agility and suppleness its scaly ancestors lacked. It turned about and charged. The enormous cat rolled on the ground, gripped by the two mighty jaws. Struggling furiously, the leopard managed to tear itself free. It ran off, frightened by the superiority of its adversary. The other, grunting, seized the antelope and drew it backward into the river. Presently, both had disappeared.

As it was retreating, the leopard saw Phillippe and Sir George. It stopped, its amber eyes burning at the two men.

"I will aim for the head," the Englishman said coolly.

"I'll do the same," Phillippe said.

The leopard hesitated. Fear, rage, and hunger shook its rough frame. Then, daunted by their alienness, by the eyes fixed upon it, the carbines that looked like prolonged limbs, it went looking for a more familiar prey.

19.

Life or Death

Death blew like a hot breath over the caravan. Here and there were slight movements, a harsh intake of breath by a donkey, or the strangely plaintive cry of a camel mixed with the chime of the plants. The huge flies were still buzzing around the animals. And the blacks, in spite of their faith in the chief, were casting troubled looks around them. In these looks was growing revolt, a revolt inspired by the madness of thirst.

"Bad," Kouram said. "I have just spoken to the men. There are some hotheads among them, master, men who do not like whites."

"If they prefer to die by our rifle fire, instead of from thirst, let them do so," Hareton said indifferently. "But tell them to wait for one more hour. If nothing's happened by then, we'll sacrifice a camel."

Kouram ran to carry the promise of the chief to the blacks.

Once more Hareton searched the horizon. Where *were* they? Had they reached the river, or were they roaming about, just like the caravan, in a desert even more abominable because it produced plants in abundance?

"It's disgusting," Guthrie growled. "I simply don't know if I'll be able to hold out for an hour. I'm having hallucinations, Uncle Hareton. My head is full of the bubble and splash of springs, cascades, and creeks. It's driving me mad. One more hour!" He looked at his watch, and ran a black, swollen tongue over his cracked lips.

Hareton turned toward the young girl.

133

"Don't worry about me," Muriel said. "I can wait for longer than an hour if need be."

But Phillippe's absence filled her with fear and distress. Had this mysterious and hostile land managed to trap him?

One more hour. The cruel light dazzled men and beasts. Guthrie felt as if he were walking around inside a gigantic furnace going full blast.

A black suddenly fell down on the ground, crying out plaintively. Another gestured with his knife. A loud grumbling rose around them.

Hareton cast another hopeless look over the surrounding emptiness. Nothing! Nothing but the blue and purple grass, the giant flies, the intolerable sound of bells.

"Is this really the end of us?"

Turning toward Muriel, his heart torn by remorse, he said, "What madness made me risk your young life?"

To gain time, he called a halt and had the tents set up, saying, "In ten minutes we'll kill a camel."

Under the rapidly erected tents, the whites and the blacks sought a slight coolness. Hareton designated two men to carry out the sacrifice. They came forward armed with sharp knives.

"Not yet!" Kouram cried. He bent down and put his ear to the ground.

He raised his head. "I hear the sound of large beasts trotting."

The next moment, everyone had his ear against the red earth.

Hareton spoke to the two men ready to kill the camel. "Don't make a move until I've given you a signal. . . . Well, Kouram?"

"The sound is getting nearer, master, and I think it is made by camels."

One of the blacks, grinning, said, "Yes! Camels!"

But another said, slowly and sadly, "Perhaps only wild boars."

"Where is the sound of hooves coming from, Kouram?"

Kouram pointed toward the southwest where a long rise in the ground crested to a height, about a hundred meters away.

"Very well," Guthrie said, as he climbed on the saddle of the largest camel. "If it's them, I'll raise both arms."

In spite of its exhaustion and thirst, the animal did not refuse to make an effort. It started off slowly, and many blacks, impatient, followed the giant.

Hareton lowered his binoculars and said, "If only it's not a deception." As he spoke, he looked at the men around him. All had their eyes turned toward the southwest.

However, Guthrie had now reached the beginning of the rise. The slope being gentle, the camel had no trouble climbing it, preceded by the blacks.

Hareton and Muriel waited, anguish and hope alternating with the beat of their hearts. A few more steps to go. Already the blacks were at the top, jumping up and down, shouting. But the watchers could not tell if it was with joy or despair.

Finally, Guthrie raised both his arms.

"Here they come!" Hareton cried.

He picked up his binoculars again and then he smiled. Guthrie was laughing.

"Water! They've found water!"

The entire caravan, including the animals, was suddenly running. In what seemed a short time Hareton had reached and climbed the slight incline.

Far away, in the desert of musical plants, two camels were running at full speed. Sir George and Phillippe could be seen plainly. Full water bags were shaking on the flanks of their humped beasts.

Deliriously happy, Guthrie was howling a victory chant, the blacks were shouting frenetically, and all of them were running toward the camels and their life-giving burdens.

"Is it water, at last?" Sydney roared when he was close enough.

"It's water," Sir George answered quietly as he handed him a gourd. "Over there, as Ironcastle had said, a great river flows through the solitude."

Guthrie drank as if he'd empty the gourd. The blacks were howling and jumping around, laughing like children. Hareton felt as if this were the most joyous moment in his life. "The Lord has not scorned our request."

These men were coming back to life as dry grass will become green once more after the rain. The animals were given a small share, but it would be sufficient to give them the strength to reach the river.

Having quenched his thirst, Hareton was listening without great surprise to the tale of Phillippe and Sir George.

"Samuel," he said, "had written to me of all these things. Tonight, the safari will make camp close to the great river."

All distress had vanished. The minds of the blacks, which dwelt only in the present, had forgotten their ordeal. Because the masters had once more triumphed, their faith was becoming unshakable.

20.

Close to the Lakeshore

The caravan halted a thousand paces from the river. Starlight dappled the plants and trees and spread itself subtly over the lonely expanse.

Six rocky hillocks surrounded the camp on the red earth, where only lichens, moss and primitive grass grew. The campfires leaped up toward the stars. The beasts moving about in the shadows watched the strange beings who hovered about the fire as if it were a friend.

Giant frogs and saurians lurked in the darkness. Also, jackals with copper hair, dancing hyenas, wild boars with red-dappled hair, pink hippos, stealthy antelopes, and even a bird of prey with cottony wings. Once, a giant lion with red hair came close to the shore of the river. He gazed at the camp for some time with shining red eyes, then slunk away.

"The lion has the hair of a fox," Sydney said.

"It has a strange walk," Phillippe said. "It's not quite catlike."

The camels, donkeys, and goats moved about uneasily. They could smell the watchers in the shadows, and they did not like what they smelled.

"It's not as large as the leopard we saw back at the river."

"No," Phillippe said. "And it's certainly less to be feared."

"Look out!" Guthrie shouted.

Three colossal beasts had suddenly appeared in the semi-darkness.

"Saurians," Hareton said, with a mixture of curiosity and apprehension.

"Hairy saurians," Phillippe said. "Like the one we saw in the morning. The largest is truly awesome."

In fact, one of the saurians was at least a decameter long, and its mass was close to that of a rhino. Its three eyes, the color of emeralds tinged with amber, reflected the firelight.

"It must be frightfully strong," Phillippe said.

"Good!" Guthrie growled, bringing up his elephant gun. "Nature has done a good job. Let's see what an artifact can do to nature."

The giant beast growled, sounding like a heavy waterfall. Slaver ran from its jaws.

"We are a bountiful reserve of food for it," Phillippe said. "Will it dare to attack us?"

The pyres were not close together since the caravan had not managed to gather enough firewood to build a continuous barricade. A courageous beast could enter the camp, but it was not likely that any would attempt it. Still, many of the beasts were slowly coming nearer.

The fantastic fauna was increasing: coppery jackals, night birds of all kinds, green monkeys, bats with white heads, lizards and giant toads, sapphire-colored serpents . . . two leopards appeared on a knoll. The lion had reappeared, and other saurians were coming up from the river . . . their eyes shone like small lamps, yellow, green, red, purplish, looking intently at the fires.

One of the leopards raised its head and roared as mightily as a large lion.

"A nightmare vision," Guthrie said.

The giant saurian yawned. Its mouth looked like a huge cave, its teeth without number. It awed the humans; here was a survivor of the age of fabulous reptiles. It was now in front of the widest gorge of the camp, where the camels were snorting with fear. The monkeys and the goats were seeking shelter close to the men. Its three eyes fixed upon a dromedary, the saurian stretched himself. Slaver dripped from its jaws, a thick green fluid. The camp animals reared, bucked, brayed, bellowed, bleated.

"One of the leopards raised its head and roared."

Some of them broke their ropes and three camels crashed to the ground, tripped by their hobbles as they tried to run toward the men.

The blacks ran to quiet the animals down. For a moment, everyone was intent on the commotion.

"Look out!" Guthrie shouted.

The saurian was in the camp. It headed straight for a dromedary which, for some mysterious reason, had its preference. The other saurians moved closer.

"Since I am on the right," Phillippe said to Sir George, "I will aim to hit the right eye."

"All right! And I, the left."

Two shots sounded. The saurian screamed, then started to run around in circles. A third bullet struck its pineal eye, blinding it completely. A fourth from Phillippe, hitting a leg, drove it into the night.

The blacks fought to calm the frightened animals. The cries of the wounded saurian held the wild beasts immobile in their tracks around the camp. Then, as the two fired at the other reptiles, they ran. Over the blue expanse, the ancient splendor of the stars trembled softly.

21.

The Young Girl in the Night

During the next two days, the safari moved on without meeting any trouble. Hareton checked his compass every morning, then gave instructions for the day's march. The fertile land spawned numberless fantastic beasts: purple hippos, oversized giraffes, hairy saurians, spiders and beetles as large as birds, elephants with four tusks, climbing-fish, snakes the color of fire. The plants were even more astonishing. A mimosa-like plant increased in numbers as they progressed toward the southwest. Their variety was truly inconceivable. Some were as tall as birch, others were like beech trees, and some surpassed the sequoias of California in size and height.

Hareton had warned his companions against them. "Darnley wrote that they are all dangerous. Stay away from them."

Guthrie was curious about them. Alone, he would no doubt have inspected them closely. But he followed the orders of his chief. Whenever they walked close to the mimosas, dwarfs or giants, the leaves would contract and emit sounds like those of a zither, a lyre or a harp, according to their size.

"What makes them so dreadful?" Sydney asked. "Is it because of their darts?"

"That is enough reason to avoid them. Their sting is painful; they give you a sort of madness. You can see that our animals are avoiding any contact with them."

"What should we do? If they get thick enough to prevent our movement. . . ."

141

"It seems they don't want that," Hareton said. "They are leaving free spaces . . . but why?"

He reread Samuel Darnley's notes. Then the sky darkened suddenly. Immense clouds arose from the depths, and the safari was enveloped in a kind of St. Elmo's fire.

"We are going to have a beautiful storm," Sir George said.

Spiral winds were rising. The air glimmered with copper and jade. A furious life exulted in the elements. Lightning cracked the sky; the men felt some unknown and obscure will of the mineral kingdom.

Then the water came down, fluttering, life-giving, mother to all things that grow and die.

The tents had been set up. The animals, unsheltered, were moving to and fro in the gusts of wind. They leaped whenever the thunder sounded, as if lions were roaming the clouds.

"Ah, how I love the storm!" Guthrie shouted, while he breathed the humid air voluptuously. "It gives me ten lives."

"It more often brings death," Sir George said.

"All things bring death! The idea is to choose, my friend."

"We do not choose. We are chosen."

All around the camp, wild beasts stampeded by. A herd of giraffes, elephants showing their rocky backs for a moment, giant lizards seeking deep holes, a rhinoceros thundering like a falling boulder, wild boars squealing fearfully, antelopes with a scared lion in their midst.

"There is no longer any difference between hunted and hunter," Phillippe said as he stood close to Muriel.

However, the celestial manifestations were already diminishing. Holes appeared among the clouds, and the rain was dwindling.

And then, the eternal furnace of the sun reappeared.

"There is the monster," Guthrie growled.

"The true Father," Sir George said.

The end of the drama came abruptly. The earth drank the water, and presently there was only mud.

"We can start off now," Hareton said in a tired voice. He began to walk heavily.

"All of a sudden, I feel very tired," Guthrie said.

"That's strange," Sir George said. "I suddenly feel completely exhausted, too."

Phillippe was silent, but it seemed to him that the weight of his body had doubled.

Hareton gave the order to leave. They did so, but painfully. The men were laggard, the animals breathed heavily, moving with excessive slowness.

"What's the matter?" Guthrie asked.

He had trouble speaking, and he moved like a man in the grip of extreme sluggishness.

The others seemed too tired to answer him. For half an hour, the caravan stumbled wearily along. All around it, isles of mimosas were increasing in such numbers as to make crossing difficult. Whenever, inadvertently, someone touched one of these plants, the leaves shook in a strange way. That phenomenon was even more striking when a tree was touched; the boughs would undulate like a nest of snakes.

"I can't go on," Guthrie said with weak anger. "It's as if I were dragging around weights of lead. Uncle Hareton, don't your notes tell you anything about this? Is it a sort of paralysis? Is it because of these damned plants?"

"I don't feel numb—as if it were paralysis," Hareton said. "No, it's not a form of paralysis . . . my ideas are clear, my feelings normal. It's only this unbearable heaviness. It seems as if we weighed more."

"Yes," Sir George said. "That's exactly it. Everything feels normal except for this heaviness."

"I seem to weigh five hundred pounds," Guthrie said. "You didn't answer, Uncle Hareton. Is this caused by the plants . . . and why?"

"I think it's the plants," Hareton said, shuddering. "And you know it well. Here, all things depend on them. I would only like to understand *what they want* . . . or in what way we are threatening them."

"There isn't a single animal to be seen," Phillippe said.

It was true. No mammal, no bird, no reptile was in

sight. Even the insects had disappeared. And at every step
they felt heavier.

The camels were the first to halt. They cried out discor-
dantly and then became silent. Then they lay down and
became motionless. The donkeys soon followed suit,
though the goats continued to move around slowly.

Hareton summoned enough energy to cry out, "What in
God's name is going on?"

His speech was now as slow as his movements, but his
touch and sight seemed untroubled, and his thinking processes were not hindered. Guthrie sat down, then lay flat on
his back. Less affected, Phillippe and Sir George were nevertheless near collapse. Only Muriel showed more resistance. However, she was unable to take a step without great
effort.

"Yes, what do *they* want?" Phillippe asked. "What have
we done to them or what are they afraid of?"

"And who are *they?*" Muriel said.

"You know," Phillippe said, but he did not offer to explain.

A forest of giant mimosas, exhaling a chilly breath of
mystery and menace, towered before them. Surely, Hareton
thought, it must have existed long before the Assyrian
kings and the Chaldean shepherds. Ten civilizations had
come and gone since their seeds had first burst from the
nourishing earth.

"Are the plants stopping us?" Hareton asked himself.
"Then, perhaps if we go back . . . ?"

But they couldn't retreat. Their legs refused to go much
farther in any direction. Whenever they tried to speak, the
sounds came out so slowly they became incomprehensible.
All of the pack animals had collapsed. Only their eyes
showed any signs of life, and these expressed great terror.

Night was approaching. A red and mournful night. Driving herself by willpower, Muriel had managed to crawl as
far as the provisions crates and had brought back smoked
meat and biscuits. In vain. No one was hungry; all were intent upon the vanishing sun. Night fell. A pink crescent began to light the surroundings weakly. Far away, very far
away, jackals were howling and yelping.

They thought of how defenseless they were. Wild beasts could eat them alive. But no animal shape appeared over the grass, on the shore, or at the edge of the forest. Fatigue, utter fatigue, dominated all sensations and all thoughts. By the time the crescent had reached the horizon, men and beasts were asleep under the trembling grace of the constellations.

Near the middle of the night, Muriel awoke. The moon had disappeared. The whiteness of the stars was like throbbing snow. The young woman arose, painfully shaken by fever but infused with an energy that seemed to originate from outside herself. Was it from the forest? She looked at her companions spread out in the ash-gray glow. Suddenly, she was overwhelmed with the feeling that *it was up to her to save them*. That sentiment excluded all logic; it suddenly came to life within her like compulsions of creatures that live only by instinct. She did not even try to reason it out.

In the grip of a semi-delirium, fighting against her still almost-overpowering weakness, she set off in the direction of the Southern Cross. Every now and then, she was forced to stop. Her head weighed heavily on her neck, like a block of granite. Often, she had to crawl. No matter how tired she was, her enthusiasm did not falter. She murmured to herself from time to time, "I *must* save them!"

She hoped that, somehow, she could get out of this lotusland danger zone. She forgot that she would then be alone in a land of canivores. Here, the strange solitude persisted; no beast could be seen in the limitless plain.

Many hours went by, each minute like an hour. Yet, she had not traveled more than a mile. Suddenly, she had a delicious feeling. The heaviness vanished. Once more, Muriel was in control of her body. She hastened to put even more distance between her and the deadly forest.

Then a new worry began to gnaw at her. The world of animals had returned. Jackals, furtive as phantoms, scudded by. A hyena limped around in the shadows, and giant toads sprang on the wet grass. Nocturnal birds of prey flew by on downy wings.

Everywhere was life, restless, swarming. Everywhere the

same agitation which, through countless ages, never ceases
to mix stubborn growth with ferocious destruction.

Heavy breathing, mysterious cries, leaves brushing together, the irregular laugh of the hyena, the abrupt yelps of
the jackal. . . . Muriel's only weapon was a revolver, but
she did not consider going back. The exaltation that had
carried her this far persisted. It was transforming itself into
a sort of confused drunkenness, no doubt a reaction to her
restored freedom and bodily energy.

Occasionally, she shivered with fear. The jackals cautiously trailing her were the symbol of all those who, on
this savage Earth, watch every living thing to destroy and to
devour it. Eternal hunger, embodied in the shape of jackals, threatened her.

Dawn was approaching when a voice pierced the silence
of the surrounding area. Muriel saw a long blue form glid-
ing stealthily among the high stalks of grass. Its eyes shone
with an emerald light. Muriel froze, not to become incon-
spicuous, but because terror congealed her flesh.

The jackals had stopped, ears stiff, resentful at losing
this prey yet ready to seize a chance to recover it. An immense solitude bore down upon her. She had never felt so
alone nor known how cruel this world was.

The revolver in her hand, she murmured, "God Almighty, You are my strength and my shield!"

In the blue night, the human eyes held those of the ferocious blue beast. Muriel was ready for battle. The great
cat, spread out full-length, was flowing toward her like water seeking a lower level; its fluid body headed toward her,
the fleshy lowlands.

22.

The Scaly Men

When Hareton opened his eyes at dawn, he lay for a while in a torpor alive with hallucinations. A mist floated before his eyes. His companions, including the ape, still slept.

Yet vague shapes were moving about inside the tent, like shadows on a wall. His bleary eyesight cleared, and then he could make out their forms. Startled, he woke up completely. Were they beasts? Were they men? They stood upright, even though their legs ended in boarlike hooves, legs like those of lizards. Their bodies were covered with translucid scales mixed with greenish hair, and their heads were unlike anything human or animal. Shaped like cylinders, with a sort of mossy cone on top, they were the color of green malachite. The triangle-shaped mouth seemed to have three lips. The nose was merely three elliptical holes. The eyes were at the bottom of cavities, the edges of which were sawtooth-shaped. Eyes which shone with a variable phosphorescence, purple, orange and yellow. The hands had four claws opposable to three others.

Hareton tried getting up, but without success. Many lianas fine as strings held his limbs tightly. They stretched slightly when the American made an effort. Ironcastle's astonishment did not last. As his head cleared, he re-read mentally the notes of Samuel Darnley. These fantastic beings were sentient, in a sense the Homo sapiens of this land.

He tried to talk to them. "What do you want?"

At the sound of his voice, cavernous eyes turned toward

him. They uttered low whistles that resembled the cry of blackbirds and the sound of far-off ferryboat whistles.

The noise awoke Phillippe first. Sir George opened his eyes a minute later, along with Guthrie. All three were also bound. In the nearby tents, the laments of the blacks were heard.

"What is this?" Guthrie cried furiously.

His mighty muscles were stretching the lianas so much that one could almost have believed that he would free himself. Ten scaly men ran to the giant but stopped when they saw that he was not able to break his bonds.

"Where do these things come from?" he howled. "By comparison, the Stunted Men are beautiful angels!"

"They are men, or almost," Hareton said. "And we are completely at their mercy—if they have any."

The blacks were crying out mournfully, and the ape was growling loudly.

"They are prisoners also."

He looked around, paled, and said, "Oh, my God! Where's Muriel? Have they carried her off? Muriel! Muriel!"

Phillippe wept with anger and frustration. Tears welled in Ironcastle's eyes.

"What do these lemurs want?" Guthrie said after a long silence.

They soon found that the "lemurs" were pseudo-humans. One by one, the whites, the ape, and most of the blacks were skillfully and methodically loaded on camels. Their clawlike hands were extraordinarily dexterous. Guthrie was shouting insults, while Sir George, impassive, growled, "Where are they taking us?"

Then they did something completely unexpected. They untied Kouram and four other blacks, afterward gesturing at the tents and animals.

Kouram understood. He said to Hareton, "Master, should we obey them?"

Ironcastle didn't hesitate long. The scaly men held the lives of the prisoners in their hands, and any resistance might result in a massacre. It was best to gain as much time as possible.

"Obey them."

Kouram said, "It will be as *Doomballa* decrees." He ordered the tents taken down. When all was ready for the departure, he led the caravan, guided by the gestures of the captors.

One of them, even more scaly and greener than the others, seemed to be their chief. About fifty pseudo-humans walked on each side of the caravan. Approximately twenty preceded it, and forty brought up the rear.

Occupied with concern for Muriel, Hareton and Maranges cared little about what was happening to them. Guthrie was only beginning to get hold of himself. Sir George, however, watched everything attentively. The intelligence of the lemurs was evident, their discipline perfect, their language well developed. The chief's finely modulated whistles sufficed to make his orders understood. He only used gestures and signs to communicate with Kouram. Somehow, he had understood that Kouram was the leader of the blacks.

"On top of that," the Britisher thought, "he's taken care to avoid freeing any of the whites. He knows, instinctively or otherwise, that they are different from the blacks and perhaps more dangerous."

The expedition walked parallel to the forest for many hours. Then the mimosas became sparse, replaced by pines, ferns, and a sort of bright green moss.

The scaly men kept urging the camels to maintain a trot.

"Where the devil are they taking us?" Guthrie asked. He was now observing what went on with as much care as Sir George.

"They are taking us *home,* I presume," the Englishman answered. "You'll notice that they're now paying no attention to the plants. Back there, they were careful not to brush against trees or even bushes."

"There isn't a single mimosa in this place," Hareton said. "And most of the vegetation seems primitive, mainly cryptogams or gymnosperms."

"That doesn't indicate anything about our fate," Sydney said.

"They haven't killed us," Sir George said quietly. "They

are going to a lot of trouble to take us with them, as well as our animals."

"And our provisions!"

"It's quite possible that they aim to keep us alive."

"At what price?" Guthrie said, scowling.

"I suppose that they intend to use us for their own purposes—whatever those might be."

"Damn it! What proof have we got that we won't supply the main course of a feast? Why shouldn't these jokers be cannibals, just like our friends the Goura-Zannkas? In that case, we haven't avoided anything by making it easy for them!"

The moor widened, and the mossy growths became enormous. The pines were now merely stunted bushes. The ferns grew in arborescent clumps harboring strange opossums, hairy birds the size of bustards, and large worms the color of rusty steel wire.

Hareton was now observing the scaly men with as much care as Sir George. Their armament was bizarre. They carried a sort of spiral harpoon, made of red stone, a plate cut in the shape of a half-moon and, in a leather bag, round spiked red projectiles. These resembled small bears. The effectiveness of these projectiles became evident when a herd of boars trotted by. Three, struck by the hurled "bear cubs," rolled about on the ground and then died. The weapons were evidently coated with poison.

"You see that they are men and even *clever* men," Sir George said to Sydney.

"What prevents some beasts from being as clever as men?" the giant grumbled. "Call them anything you like, but not men!"

Around noon the chief of the expedition gave the signal to halt. They stopped in the shadow of ferns as tall as plane trees. Their thick leaves cast a refreshing shade.

Kouram got permission to communicate with his masters and with the blacks that were still bound.

"Do you understand them, Kouram?" Ironcastle asked.

"Often, master. I know that they want me to give you something to eat and drink."

His voice was slow, sad, and tired. It was obvious that

he expected to die soon. His faith in the whites had vanished. They had gotten him safely through one horror after another, but the scaly men were too much even for Ironcastle and the herculean Guthrie.

Aided by his free companions, he helped his masters to eat and drink first. Afterward, he took care of the blacks.

The halt did not last long. The strange safari got back on the road and once more the terrain changed. Rocky hills rose abruptly from the plain, and soon they were in a gloomy narrow gorge, its walls as red as fresh blood.

When sunset neared, another halt was called. The prisoners viewed with melancholy the immense crimson valley enclosed by high cliffs, exitless except for the pass through which they had emerged.

"Do these creatures live here?" Guthrie said. "I see no trace of any dwellings."

"I presume that they live *in* the rock," Sir George said.

The whistles of the chief interrupted him. The scaly men formed a circle around the caravan. Suddenly, others popped out of holes at the base of the red cliffs.

Piercing whistles answered the chief's. The camels having been relieved of their bags and crates of supplies, the bound men were dragged off and dumped onto the ground.

Half a dozen scaly men brought dry wood and made a fire on which they sprinkled a yellowish liquid. The stuff sputtered, crackled, and then poured out clouds of a pleasing aroma.

"Things don't look good," Hareton said grimly, as he saw the flames leap up. "My friends, just in case, let's say good-bye."

Their captors were chasing the beasts of burden toward the other end of the circular valley.

"I feel that I got you into this," Ironcastle said. "I ask for your forgiveness."

"Come on, Uncle Hareton," Guthrie said. "We are men, and we intend to take responsibility for our own actions."

Phillippe thought of Muriel and his sister Monique. Even though Muriel had somehow escaped, she would die in this hideous land. And Monique—who would take care of her?

"I don't mind dying," Sir George said. "If I could do it while fighting. But to lie here, helpless, like an animal in a slaughterhouse. . . ."

"Let's pray," Hareton said.

The flames cast an orange glow over the shadows of the rocks. The aromatic smoke was becoming thicker. As the captives breathed it, they felt their senses becoming weaker. Far away, the scaly men were moving about in a fantastic and rhythmic fashion, occasionally emitting long whistling sounds. One by one, the prisoners lost consciousness.

23.

Muriel in the Unknown

The huge feline would only have had to leap once to seize Muriel. The horde of jackals, although nearer to her, did not dare to attack her. The prey was large-bodied, and once the cat had fed to its satisfaction, there would be some meat and bones left for them. They knew their turn would come; it always did.

Two shots sounded as the cat leaped. Nevertheless, it knocked Muriel down. Sharp canines opened to close on her white throat.

At that moment, raucous cries like the howls of wolves rose over the plains. Two peculiar animals appeared on the knoll. Their scaly bodies were shaped somewhat like those of Newfoundland dogs; their cubic heads were almost as large as a lion's.

The big cat, snarling, backed away. The jackals, yelping, were running away. The monstrous beasts approached. When they were only a few paces away, the feline ran away as fast as it could go. Muriel rose. An even more mysterious danger threatened her. These creatures looked as unreal, as mythical as winged bulls, unicorns, fauns, and mermaids. Muriel crossed her arms and waited for the attack, knowing that they could tear her apart with ease.

But there was no attack. Two steps away from the young girl, the beasts stopped. Almost immediately, other beings appeared. But these belonged to the known universe. They were three black men, very tall and *armed with carbines*. Their bearing was so similar to that of the blacks in the safari that, for a moment, she thought it was they. Then she realized that she was mistaken. They were dressed in cloth made of something like unpolished glass, but glass as soft as linen or hemp. A close-fitting body garment, a short woolen cloth, falling from the waist to mid-thigh, hats with flat rims, a belt holding a knife and an axe, these constituted their apparel.

They waved, and one of them shouted in English, "No fear! Friends!"

She was too astounded to speak until they came down from the knoll.

When they were near, the one who had spoken—he looked somewhat like Kouram—said, "American?"

She was too bewildered to say anything but "Yes."

Grinning, the man said, "Me, too."

A moment of silence followed. The scaly animals moved restlessly around her. The blacks eyed her as if waiting for her to explain her presence. Suddenly, she had an inspiration. She said in a low voice, "Do you know Samuel Darnley?"

"He is my boss."

"We are looking for him."

"I thought so!" the black exclaimed. He laughed and slapped his hands together. "So, Miss . . . or Mrs . . . ?"

"Miss Ironcastle."

"Come! He's back there."

"Is it far?"

"Two hours' march."

They took her through a savanna and then crossed, with great care, a forest where baobabs and banyan trees alternated with mimosas. However, their journey was easy, the trees being far apart or forming isles that could easily be skirted.

After pausing at a broad river, they followed the banks until they came to a place where enormous stones, close to one another, allowed an easy crossing.

"We are almost there," said the one who had first spoken to Muriel.

The vegetation was becoming sparse. Red earth, bordered by a rocky wall, spread out flatly on both sides. At the end of two hours, the scaly beasts stopped and uttered their weird cries.

A tall man appeared in the shadow of the rocks. His skin was tanned almost black. His beard fell to his chest, and his hair was as blond as Muriel's. His sea-blue eyes widened when he saw Muriel, and he shouted, stupefied, "Miss Ironcastle!"

"Mr. Darnley!"

She almost fainted with joy and relief. Samuel Darnley, having stepped toward her, took her hands in his and held them tenderly. Then, worry creasing his tanned face, he said, "Hareton?"

"He's back there . . . with the expedition," she said in a shaky voice. "He and the others were overcome by a mysterious lethargy. Since yesterday, we've been unable to move. For some reason, I was able to partially overcome it."

Darnley shook his head and frowned.

"It was *their* doing," he growled. "You stepped onto a temporarily forbidden ground and *they* defended themselves."

"Who?"

"The mimosas . . . you have to know them and obey them."

"What does that mean?" she said. Suddenly, her eyes widened.

Two other blacks had just come up. With them were the creatures impossible to define. They were bipeds, in some ways human. But their elephant-like feet, their saurian legs, the scales mixed with rough hair, their cylinder-like heads surmounted by a mossy cone, their triangle-shaped mouths, their eyes sunken in deep holes, shining with a multi-hued phosphoresence, these repulsed and at the same time fascinated her. She felt as if she were looking at a Martian zoo.

"They are men," Darnley said. "Or rather, they are playing the role of men in this land. Their organism is as different from ours as that of a baboon or a dog. Don't worry about a thing, Miss. They are my allies, incapable of the slightest treason. Only those who are not yet my allies are to be feared."

He stopped, frowning. "Let's keep our minds on Ironcastle and his friends. Since you've managed, in spite of everything, to escape, it's because the accumulated energy had already diminished. Therefore, I believe our friends are already awake and walking about . . . let's go and meet them."

He quickly gave some orders to the four blacks, then spoke to the scaly men, sometimes by sign language, sometimes with strange whistles.

In a quarter of an hour, the expedition was ready. The blacks were armed with rifles, the scaly ones with a sort of red harpoon and a plate-like shield in the shape of a half-circle. Leather bags hung from their waists.

"Let's go," Darnley said.

He was silent for a long time. Muriel kept waiting for him to offer an explanation. Finally, as if recalling that she was with him, he started. Blinking his eyes he said, "There's no reason to worry. Believe me, *they* are *not* killers. Even when heaviness or sleep last awhile, little harm is done. I've seen animals asleep for three or four days without suffering any harm."

"But," Muriel said, "what if, during their sleep, some man-eating beasts invaded the camp? There are some frightful beasts in this land."

"Don't be afraid. Our friends will wake up automatically before any dangerous animal gets near them. The end of sleep follows the end of the heavy feeling by about an hour. During that hour, any area subject to that phenomenon is inviolable, except for these sentient beings. They are less subject to the influence. But most of the surrounding tribes are my friends."

"What would they do?" Muriel said. "I mean those who aren't your allies?"

"I don't really know. Different tribes have different customs, different attitudes. Furthermore, there are two races here. The most dangerous, however, is by far the least numerous."

A shadow passed over his eyes but, smiling, he said, "It's almost certain that we'll find them safe and sound."

"Is it dangerous to penetrate this forest?" she said.

"There are many such forests in this country. If we re-

spect them, keep our distance, and if we are not careless . . .
if we don't cross forbidden zones, it's possible to travel
through the forest."

"How can we recognize the forbidden zones?"

"The heaviness is a sign. As soon as you feel it, you
must stop and wait . . . or else go around the obstacle. A
mysterious anguish is another sign. You begin to choke,
and you find yourself in the grip of sudden fear. Sometimes, it's a fever. It gets worse as you progress into the
forbidden region. Sometimes, it also happens that you are
repulsed."

"Are there boundaries that we must never cross?"

"No. There are simply acts that we must never accomplish. You will soon learn to recognize them."

They had gone beyond the knoll where the blue cat had
attacked Muriel. Now they had to locate her trail, since she
did not remember where she had walked in this area. The
scaly men and the pseudo-dogs got to work tracking. Eventually, they stopped, seemingly at a dead-end. They spread
out. stooping and sniffing.

"The safari stopped here," Darnley said. "Here is the
proof."

He showed her traces left by the stakes of the tents, a tin
can, a frayed piece of rope.

One of the blacks shouted something, and the others ran
to him. The scaly men were searching around in the dirt.

"Boss," the American black said, "*they* came here. See
the footprints."

Darnley suddenly looked worried.

"No signs of a struggle?"

"None, sir."

The black looked first at Darnley, then at Muriel.

"Tell us, I beg you," Muriel said.

Samuel made a fatalistic gesture. It would serve no pur-
pose to beat around the bush; the young girl would always
imagine the worst.

"*They* made them all prisoners."

"Who do you mean, *they*?" Muriel said.

"They who are like men."

A dark fear froze Muriel. Visions of death rushed at her.

"I don't believe they'll kill them," Darnley said. "At least not for a long time."

He seemed to regret having said these last words.

"We mustn't waste any more time," he added. "Let's go!"

The blacks, the animals, and the scaly ones were now following the trail as easily as if the prisoners and their captors had been visible. Swiftly, the party went through a country full of pines, ferns, and the hairy moss. The tall, treelike ferns rustled, though there was no wind.

"Do you think we're getting close?" Muriel asked hesitantly.

"Not yet," Samuel said. "They are hours ahead of us. We can't expect to reach them before dusk—if they stop!"

"And what if they don't stop?"

Darnley shrugged and rolled his eyes.

"But," Muriel said, her voice shaking, "do you hope to be able to free them before . . . ?"

"I hope so."

Seeing the forlorn face of the young girl, he thought it best to give her some details.

"In all probability, it's the people of the Red Circus. They can muster about a hundred and fifty fighting men. We are only forty, but I've sent for some reinforcements. So you must stop worrying. Ah!"

One of the blacks had just run up to signal the first halt of the captors. The terrain was now explored in all directions. Having revealed nothing important, the pursuit continued. When they reached the red gorge, they stopped. The blacks and Darnley ate a short meal. Muriel managed to swallow a few bites of a biscuit with some difficulty. The scaly men ate fern roots and a sticky paste made from lichen.

At that moment, a scaly man appeared from behind a boulder and whistled softly.

"The reinforcements are coming," Darnley said.

"My God," the girl murmured. "We'll have to *fight*?"

"Perhaps not. The People of the Red Circus know that we are better armed than they."

"They will have the rifles and the machine gun."

"But they don't know how to use them."

Cautiously, the column advanced into the gorge. Two hours before dusk, the scouts fell back. Darnley conferred with them for a few moments, then returned to Muriel. He looked very grave.

"It is the People of the Red Circus. Our scouts think they haven't been seen. However, no matter what happens, it's in the Circus that the issue will be decided. They can't abandon their fortress because of the women and children. And also, that's where they feel strongest. Let's take precautions."

He drew a flask from his pocket and poured a few drops in a tiny cup.

"It's an antidote. Go on, take it!"

Muriel swallowed the drink without hesitation. Darnley also drank. She could see the blacks and the scaly men doing the same. The blacks were using cups just like Darnley. The others were drinking from a sort of reed which held the liquid.

"Now we are protected. Let's hit the road," Darnley said.

They were moving forward more rapidly, although as cautiously as before.

Darnley said, "All the tribes know the art of causing sleep by burning or by evaporating certain substances. But they also know an antidote, and that's what we've just used. It must be taken at least half an hour in advance to give it a chance to work."

"When will we get there?"

"We're not two miles away from the Red Circus. Let me give the final orders."

He called the two blacks and some of the scaly men to him. For a few minutes, words and whistling sounds alternated.

"We're ready," the explorer said to Muriel. "Now, all we need is a little luck."

Muriel was surprised to see about fifteen scaly men climb the rocks. On reaching the top, they disappeared.

"They know all the hidden exits from the Red Circus," Darnley said.

Once more, the pace slowed. Both men and animals walked stealthily and silently. Darnley was now closer to the vanguard, but he had warned Muriel to follow him at a safe distance.

Approximately half an hour went by. Then some whistling sounds came from somewhere. Darnley and his men began to run. Muriel couldn't stop herself from following them.

Suddenly, the Red Circus was straight ahead. Smoke arose from it, spreading a fragrant smell. Hundreds of creatures were in its center, whirling in a mad dance around the prisoners, lying bound on the earth.

"My father!" Muriel shouted. And she added, in a lower tone, "Phillippe!"

Scaly men seemed to emerge from the rocks everywhere. They cast burning projectiles that blazed fiercely, producing a green smoke. Among the troops massed at the exit of the pass, about twenty scaly men were also hurling flaming missiles.

The dancers screamed and ran off in all directions, but few got far. Muriel watched them fall with a mingled joy and horror. The males looked just like Darnley's allies. Those of lower stature, with blue bags of flesh on their chests, had to be women. Of course, the more slender, very short ones, were the children.

"They are beaten," he told Muriel. "In a few minutes, they will be powerless. We took them completely by surprise."

By groups and individually, the scaly people staggered, reeled, and collapsed. Presently, the green smoke was gone, but it had claimed every one of the horde.

"Praise be the Lord," Darnley murmured. "We arrived just in time."

"My father and his friends?" Muriel said, groaning.

"There's nothing to fear. Even if I did not have what it takes to wake them up, all that would be necessary would be to wait till the narcotic had lost its effect. But I've been prepared for a long time."

Muriel ran down to her father and fell upon his body. Darnley drew a translucid flagon from one of his pockets, opened it, and plunged a thin syringe into it. He gave shots in quick succession to Ironcastle, Maranges, Curtis, Guthrie, Dick, and Patrick, then to the blacks, while his companions were untying their bonds.

Ironcastle woke first, shortly followed by Maranges and Sir George. For a few minutes, their thoughts were hazy and slow. Finally, Hareton's eyes lost their glaze. Seeing his daughter, he gave a great cry of joy. On seeing Darnley, he looked puzzled for a moment. But he soon understood what happened.

Darnley helped him rise, then embraced him. "It must have been God himself who directed Muriel to me," he said.

In turn, Phillippe and Sir George regained full consciousness.

"Safe! You're safe!" Phillippe whispered to Muriel.

Guthrie was the last one to wake up. Seemingly unaware of what had happened, unaccountably finding himself unbound, he leaped up roaring, grabbed an unconscious scaly man, and lifted him high to dash him upon the ground.

"Stop!" Hareton yelled. "They're beaten! We're all safe!"

Guthrie, shaking the fog from his head, looked around. Then he dropped the body and leaped with whoops of joy upon Muriel. Around and around he twirled her while she shouted at him to stop. Finally, laughing, he released her.

"Here is my friend Darnley," Ironcastle said. "It's because of him that we've managed to avoid this."

Sir George said, "What peril have we been protected from? Death? Something worse?"

Darnley smiled and said, "I don't know. In any case, not an imminent death. When we intervened, you were about to become their prey . . . in a very peculiar fashion. They don't eat flesh . . . but they drink blood. When they practice this with their own kind or with animals of this land, they rarely cause death. But perhaps you would have become too weakened and so unable to recuperate. All beings here are used to very long periods of fasting and to considerable loss of blood."

"Then these brutes are vampires," Sydney growled, disgustedly.

"Not in the legendary sense," Darnley said, and he laughed.

24.

The Vegetable Kingdom

"This fish resembles speckled trout in an astonishing way," Guthrie said between enthusiastic bites.

"Yes," Darnley replied. "As far as its taste goes. But as a species and even as a genus, it's another thing altogether. It is closer to a cyprinid. In fact, it has no place in any known classification."

"Anyway, I'll give it a good classification in my stomach," Guthrie said.

The guests were eating lunch in a hall of granite, the furniture of which was made by the genius of the blacks, the scaly men, and the energy of Darnley. Comfort was not entirely absent; the seats were upholstered. As for the knives, forks, spoons, plates and pots, the safari had supplied these.

Through open windows, they could see an expanse of red rock, followed by one of pines, ferns, giant mosses, and monstrous lichens.

The travelers, having gotten here three or four hours before dawn, and being frightfully tired, had slumbered like hibernating bears.

"No mimosas here?" Hareton said.

"No. This is home," Darnley said. "Those pine trees, ferns, moss, and lichens are as harmless here as in our respective homelands. The preeminence of the vegetation begins with angiosperms and, as you already know, reaches all its profusion with the mimosas."

The blacks had brought in two legs of roasted antelope, which drew the eager and respectful look of Sydney.

"Haven't the animals," asked Sir George, "and those

half-men that took us prisoners, any means of defense against the plants?"

"Against the superior plants, or at least the plants that are superior *here*, they have no defense except staying away or else a strict obedience *to the laws and decrees.* . . . Everything is allowed, as I've said before, where the gymnosperms are concerned and even the cryptogams. But as soon as you get to the monocotyledons, danger begins and keeps on getting worse after that, following a rather regular pattern. I don't know why the most powerful plants are the mimosas, rather than another kind of ancient dicotyledon.

"At first, we'd be tempted to believe that inferior plants must perish. Rather than that, they remain prosperous, and they occupy almost as much ground as the others. I think I've discovered the cause. The higher plants exhaust the soil, and they need to alternate with inferior plants. The latter make for a more favorable soil, at times by gradually replacing the dominant plants, or at other times by growing on the same ground. In return, the dominant species of plants invade the ground modified by the others. It's especially true where great, long-lived trees are concerned that primitive plants grow all around. In that case, their presence is useful to perpetually maintain a good, productive soil."

"That would have been sufficient to fill with admiration the writers that used to celebrate the harmony of nature," Phillippe said.

"Yes," Darnley answered. "And this time they would have been right."

"What interests me most of all," Guthrie said, helping himself to a large slice of antelope, "is knowing the relation between the plants and the animals . . . and particularly with those monsters that almost drank our blood. . . . After all, the animals did manage to stay alive. . . ."

"For many reasons, and there are two main ones. First of all, in the territory of the cryptogams and gymnosperms, men and beasts live as we do at home. They use plants the way they wish. Those who are almost men could even have an agriculture, with the restriction that their lands are al-

ways under the threat of an invasion by the plants that cannot be domesticated and which are invincible.

"The second reason is that, *if they obey the laws,* they
are not forbidden to circulate among the superior plants or
even to use them for food. There are periods when the herbivores can reap the gramineous plants with as much im-
punity as they do the moss, the lichens, the ferns and the
young pines. They are warned when they can't do that.
First, by the taste of the plants, which causes them to feel an
unbearable aversion. Second, by the poison they secrete
whenever it's necessary. Furthermore, there are fruits that
are sacrificed, I don't know for what reason. They are recognized by their smell and by their feel. The forbidden
grains and fruits cause an immediate discomfort and dif-
fuse a bitter smell. No animal will ever mistake it. All
things considered, animal life is less precarious here than
under human domination. It is only subject to different re-
strictions, compensated by real advantages."

"We can already see," Sir George said, "that laws have a
much better chance of being observed due to the fact that
some of them cannot be transgressed unless the deed is
punished by death."

"In certain surroundings, none of them can be transgressed," Darnley said. "Wherever the mimosas are in
great numbers, the rule allows for not even the slightest
disobedience. Even elsewhere, transgression brings punish-
ment so harsh and fast as to force the animals and the scaly
men to obey. Merely touching any mimosa causes unease
or pain. If the mimosa is tall, and therefore older, it knows
how to keep you at a distance by using a repulsive force
the nature of which I don't understand. You've seen that,
with the help of an acceleration of energy (I call it that because it resembles gravity, which is almost certainly caused
by a form of acceleration), you've seen that the plants can
make all movement impossible. They also have at their disposal, and you've seen that, the power of putting you to
sleep. They know how to coordinate their energies perfectly. No plant by itself, even if it had been a giant mimosa,
would have managed to paralyze your caravan at a distance. On top of that, when the mimosas are near certain

plants which are in danger they can come to their assist-
ance by feeding them through the ground radiations or de-
fensive fluids."

"In the message that you sent me," Ironcastle said, "you
mention that you don't know if the acts carried out by your
plants find their origin in some form of intelligence. It
seems to me, rather, that all this is in direct relation to it."

"Perhaps . . . and then, perhaps not. There is, in the
actions of the plants, a certain logic. But that logic so closely corresponds to circumstances, it is so identical in quality
and quantity, when identical perils have to be faced. In the
end it is so capricious that I can't compare it *as such* to human intelligence."

"So it would be a sort of instinct?"

"No, not that either. Instinct is frozen. Its presence ends
in repetitive acts, while the actions of the dominant plants
manifest themselves according to diverse events. It is an
answer to the spontaneous occurrence, whatever the occurrence may be, providing it's a menace. In a sense, the reaction of the plants seems like a mineral phenomenon, but
with a spontaneous reaction and with a diversity that resemble intelligence. Thus, it's a manifestation that cannot
be classified."

"You believe, without any restriction, that the role of the
plants unerringly dominates both animals and men?"

"I am sure of it. Here, everything is subservient to the
needs of the plants that reign over all else. Animal resistance would be in vain. I have discovered no way to avoid
the norm myself."

"However, if an energetic race, showing as much crea-
tive spirit as the Anglo-Saxons, should establish itself
here?"

"I am convinced that it would have to submit itself.
Moreover, you've been able to realize, even observe partially, that the rule of the superior plants does not have the
destructive character of human rule. Animals are not threatened brutally. They are allowed to live if they obey the
law. There is no coercion and no work."

"What about evolution?"

"You've seen that it differs greatly from what it is elsewhere. Thus, reptiles aren't inferior to mammals. They are often intelligent and are covered with hair. And the pseudo-humans show some analogy with marsupials. The females have a pouch where the babies finish growing, but that pouch is different from that of the opossums. As you've noticed, the body of these beings is at once scaly and hairy. They have a sense that we do not have, which I might call a spatial sense, one which assists sight. They do not enjoy the use of articulate speech but they can express themselves perfectly with the help of modulated whistles. These simultaneously comprise high sounds, harmonies, some alternances, certain repetitions also, as well as brief notes and long ones. The number of combinations at their disposal, in all truth, is more numerous than that of our syllables. They seem to have no sense of aesthetic beauty. Men and women among them, if I dare call them that, are drawn to one another only by the qualities of the sounds which they can produce."

"Then music would decide their selection?"

"A strange music that makes no sense to our ears or to the ears of birds. However, it must hold a beauty unknown to us. Rhythms without any resemblance to ours. I've tried to form an opinion on this, a notion, no matter how vague. And I had to give it up. As far as the degree of their social development is concerned, it scarcely goes beyond the stage of the tribe. A tribe comprised of many distinct clans. I've been unable to discover any trace of religion. They know how to make weapons and tools, subtle poisons, strong soporifics, *mineral cloth* that looks more like soft felt than woven cloth. They live in the rocks, where they dig very complex caves."

"You can talk to them?"

"With signs. Our senses are too limited to adapt themselves to their language. I've put together a vocabulary of signs with the help of which we can exchange any practical idea. I've been unable to go beyond the stage of pre-abstracts. By that I mean the abstraction that has to do with daily events. As far as any form of abstraction is concerned: nothing."

"Are you safe living in their midst?"

"Completely. They know nothing of crime, meaning disobedience to the rules of the race or to accepted behavior. From that, unusual loyalty springs forth, as sure and infallible as gravity. Any alliance with them is irrevocable."

"In that case," Guthrie said, "they are better than we!"

"Morally speaking, no doubt. In any case, the morality of this land is superior to that of ours . . . for there is a sort of reflex morality in the domination of the mimosas, and any destruction is limited to the strictest needs. Even among carnivorous beasts, you never find any that waste flesh. Besides, many carnivores are simply blood-eaters; they take blood from their victims without killing them, or even exhausting them."

There was a long silence while the blacks brought unknown fruits, reminiscent of raspberries, but raspberries as large as oranges.

"All things considered, you've not been unhappy here?"

"I've never thought either about happiness or unhappiness. A permanent curiosity keeps my thinking processes active, as well as my sentiments and my impressions. I don't believe that I'll ever have the courage to leave this land."

Hareton sighed. A devouring curiosity was also awakening in his breast but his eyes turned in the direction of Muriel and Phillippe. The future of these young creatures was elsewhere.

"You are fated to remain here for the next four months," Darnley said. "The rainy season is almost upon us and will begin in a few weeks. It would make your trip impossible."

Hareton, halfway consoled, thought that during the four months he would be able to gather unique data and to make a report unmatched in the annals of science.

"Besides," Samuel went on, speaking rather to Sydney, Sir George and Phillippe because he knew Hareton to be disinterested, "you won't go away broke. There are enough gold and precious stones in the red earth to make a thousand fortunes."

Guthrie loved too many things to be unconcerned about

wealth. Sir George had inherited from his uncle, Sir Henry Curtis, the famous explorer, a baronet's title and the estate of Brayley Hall in Yorkshire. But the inheritance had not been enough to repair the ruins of two estates inherited from his father: Hornfield and Hawktower. Now he could rebuild them and refurnish them splendidly. Phillippe was thinking of Muriel and Monique. He would not be asking Muriel to marry a poverty-stricken man now, and his sister could have a magnificent dowry.

Darnley, however, was now looking at them so peculiarly, with such a mysterious, somehow menacing expression, that they became apprehensive.

"What is it?" Hareton said. "You've been holding something back, haven't you? And you're not sure you should tell us about it?"

"It's not the wealth I promised you," Darnley said. "Those do exist, and you will go home wealthy. But. . . ."

He was silent for a moment. Then, seeming to make a decision which had been long postponed, he said, "Very well. I might as well show you. But you must promise me, solemnly, never to reveal this to anyone else. Under no circumstances."

He looked at Hareton.

"It'll be doubly, triply difficult for you to keep quiet. By doing so, you will deprive yourself of perhaps becoming the most famous naturalist that ever lived."

"Do you mean," Hareton said, "that I cannot publish my observations? But . . . surely . . . why not? I mean, others will be coming into this territory sometime within the next few years. Africa is getting increasingly crowded. More and more unknown territory is being explored. For all we know, there may be an expedition on its way to this area right now."

"I hope not," Darnley said. "I'd like to see the plants and strange animals of this land left in peace for at least a few years. Say, two or three. After that, it won't matter."

He paused, looking sad, and then said, "By then, they will all be dead!"

"What?" Hareton said. "But. . . ."

"We'll leave tomorrow on a short but fascinating, or should I say incredible, trip," Darnley said. "In the meantime, I will try to explain, to arm you with the knowledge you will need to understand what I am going to show you."

25.

The King Is Dead

"We have several kilometers to go," Darnley said. "But I want to show you something first."

They were all there, the whites, the blacks, and some of their weird allies. Nearby, on top of a rounded hill of red earth, a mimosa stood. It towered two hundred feet but, unlike most of the others of its kind, seemed dead. It was dry, brittle, riddled with holes made by a woodpecker-type of bird.

Darnley pointed to a spot at the foot of the hill and ordered some of the blacks to start digging there. As shovels were applied, Hareton inspected the soil.

"It's loose," he said. "It's been dug up before."

"Who did that?" Guthrie said.

"The natives used to. But they've quit, since they no longer get what they dug for," Darnley said.

Within half an hour an oblong trench 180 centimeters long, 60 centimeters wide, and 90 centimeters deep lay before them. Darnis, one of Darnley's American blacks, climbed out of the excavation. The whites crowded around to look down into it.

A root as wide as the trench lay half-exposed on the bottom. It was gray and dry and brittle-looking. Protruding from it near the center of the length was a reddish object.

"It looks like one of the granite tips the Stunted Men used for spearheads!" Muriel said.

"It is," Darnley said. "Rather, it's a member of the semimineral specimens the Stunted Men, and other sapient species, use. Only, if it were pulled from the root, it would be half-formed. The root died while the specimen was half-done."

"Ah!" Hareton said. "Then that explains why the spearheads were of granite, a rock totally useless as a cutting weapon. I wondered how the Stunted Men could flake them into shape, since granite does not lend itself to flaking, like flint or chert."

"It's not granite," Darnley said. "It just looks like it. But if you were to examine it under a microscope, you would see the difference between granite, an igneous stone, and this. For one thing, it is as hard as steel and has, in fact, more ferrous content than granite."

"Then," Hareton said, "this is one of the artifacts produced by the underground system of roots of the vegetable kingdom? You told us about it last night, but I'm afraid that it didn't fully sink in."

"It's not so much a kingdom as a king," Darnley said. "The vegetable kingdom here is really a single entity. All the roots originated at that dead specimen of mimosa you see on the hilltop. This whole area, under the surface, is one vast complex of connected roots.

"And the spearheads are, or were, only one type of artifact used by the sentients hereabouts. Some grow, or grew, underground and had to be dug up. Others actually grew on branches, like stone fruit. But the natives tell me that was some time ago. Though the entity is dead only at the central part, the roots are dying outward. They finally ceased producing the artifacts about four years ago."

"Then the artifact-growing was one aspect of the symbiosis between the vegetable entity and the animal life here?" Hareton said.

"Yes."

Guthrie said, "Too bad it didn't produce gold and silver, too. It could have sucked up or dissolved the precious metals and produced them in nodules, or something like that, couldn't it? Imagine, a tree bearing golden apples? Hey, do you suppose that's where the original myth, the Greek story about such trees, originated from?"

"Perhaps," Darnley said. "The natives themselves have a legend that there once was such a tree in this area."

Darnley then led the party to the foot of the hill. He stopped and pointed at a dark circular area with a diameter about a decameter long.

"That is where you dug?" Hareton said.

"Yes. The natives objected to my doing so. They said the hill was taboo. So I had to start the digging by myself. After awhile, when they saw I wasn't struck down by darts from the tree, they decided that the king was dead. Or, at least, its brain or heart was dead. And they pitched in to help me."

Darnley gave a brief order. The work went apace, with five shifts each energetically digging until panting, unable to keep up the speed. Where the red earth had not been dug previously, it was hard. A cave entrance was opened, a wide and high shaft made. Then, suddenly, the shovels went through a wall into air.

Though Hareton's party had been partially prepared, they were awed when they went into the natural cavern which enclosed the deep trunk and the roots like a globe of air. Hareton and Darnis turned on their flashlights, and they all stood still, staring.

The trunk of the mimosoid extended halfway down the hole. From there six great roots grew out and then downward, like arches, and plunged into the ground.

Under the trunk, surrounded by the curving roots, visible between the openings, was something that glittered and flashed as the beams passed over it.

"It looks like a crystal star," Muriel said quietly. "Or the outlines of one. A skeleton of a star, rather."

"It *is* a skeleton," Darnley said. "But it's not of bone. It's mineral, crystalline. The body it once supported, however, must have been vegetable. The . . . what shall I call it? . . . the mineral-vegetable king buried itself here . . . oh, I don't know how many millennia ago . . . and from its body grew the first mimosoid. The roots also grew, and spread subterraneously, and parts extended into the air. They became the many types of trees and bushes you passed on your way in.

"All of these are parts, organs, I don't know what, of the

king. Then the king died, and the organs, the limbs, are dying outward from the central body."

"But," Hareton said, "where did it come from? It's surely not of terrestrial origin?"

"Of course not. It came from somewhere out there. From Mars? From the planet of a distant star? We may never know. Anyway, travel from some planet or star it did, but in what? I suspect that the vehicle it used was also buried here. I speculate that the king sat, or squatted, or whatever, in the center of the buried spaceship. Then it ate the spaceship."

"What?" Guthrie said, and he laughed, though not very loudly.

"There are a few small pieces of some strange material here and there. The edges look as if they've been eaten with acid. The digestive juices of the king from the stars?

"Anyway, the vehicle disappeared, and the entity grew through the centuries, perhaps through a millenium. Then it could extend its body no more. Why, I don't know. I imagine that it had thought that it could grow over the entire planet. And the life it found here it would change to resemble the life of the planet of its origin. It, in other words, was adapting Earth to it, not itself to Earth.

"By some means, the chemicals which its extensions fed to the animal life? . . . who knows . . . it effected strange changes in the animal life within its influence. Hence, all that you have encountered here, the seemingly unnatural zoosphere.

"But Earth was too strong for the alien life. And Earth, Mother Earth, conquered.

"Which means that all will revert within a comparatively short time to the terrestrial, to the natural. That is, what is natural for this planet."

"This is infinitely more valuable than all the gold and silver in the earth," Hareton said, almost choking with awe. "This is a revelation of the vastness of space, of the riches of life which the planets throughout the universe, worlds on end, bear on their fertile breasts. This glimpse of life infinite and ubiquitous, of unimaginable variety, has been given to us. We must treasure it as a treasure beyond calculation. It bears testimony to the existence of the Creator and of the Creator's works. Though we remain only human to the eyes of others, we know that we have somehow partaken of the Creator's essence.

"It's like a sort of visual communion."

"Then, that being so," Muriel said, "let's seal up the tomb and leave its occupant untouched. Let us also seal our lips. There is something sacred about this. To let the world know of it would mean its profanation."

"Agreed," Guthrie said. "However, there is nothing sacred about gold and silver. We can take that."

Guthrie was always eminently practical.

DRAY PRESCOTT

The great novels of Kregen, world of Antares

<table>
<tr><td>☐</td><td>TRANSIT TO SCORPIO</td><td>(#UY1169—$1.25)</td></tr>
<tr><td>☐</td><td>WARRIOR OF SCORPIO</td><td>(#UY1212—$1.25)</td></tr>
<tr><td>☐</td><td>SWORDSHIPS OF SCORPIO</td><td>(#UY1231—$1.25)</td></tr>
<tr><td>☐</td><td>PRINCE OF SCORPIO</td><td>(#UY1251—$1.25)</td></tr>
<tr><td>☐</td><td>ARMADA OF ANTARES</td><td>(#UY1227—$1.25)</td></tr>
<tr><td>☐</td><td>KROZAIR OF KREGEN</td><td>(#UW1288—$1.50)</td></tr>
<tr><td>☐</td><td>SECRET SCORPIO</td><td>(#UW1344—$1.50)</td></tr>
<tr><td>☐</td><td>SAVAGE SCORPIO</td><td>(#UW1372—$1.50)</td></tr>
<tr><td>☐</td><td>CAPTIVE SCORPIO</td><td>(#UW1394—$1.50)</td></tr>
<tr><td>☐</td><td>GOLDEN SCORPIO</td><td>(#UW1424—$1.50)</td></tr>
<tr><td>☐</td><td>A LIFE FOR KREGEN</td><td>(#UE1456—$1.75)</td></tr>
<tr><td>☐</td><td>A SWORD FOR KREGEN</td><td>(#UJ1485—$1.95)</td></tr>
<tr><td>☐</td><td>A FORTUNE FOR KREGEN</td><td>(#UJ1505—$1.95)</td></tr>
<tr><td>☐</td><td>A VICTORY FOR KREGEN</td><td>(#UJ1532—$1.95)</td></tr>
</table>

Fully illustrated

DAW BOOKS are represented by the publishers of Signet and Mentor Books, THE NEW AMERICAN LIBRARY, INC.

THE NEW AMERICAN LIBRARY, INC.,
P.O. Box 999, Bergenfield, New Jersey 07621

Please send me the DAW BOOKS I have checked above. I am enclosing
$_____ (check or money order—no currency or C.O.D.'s).
Please include the list price plus 50¢ per order to cover handling costs.

Name _____

Address _____

City _____ State _____ Zip Code _____
Please allow at least 4 weeks for delivery